things i know about love

things i know about love

KATE LE VANN

EGMONT
USA
NEW YORK

EGMONT

We bring stories to life

Published in the United States of America by Egmont USA, 2010
443 Park Avenue South, Suite 806
New York, NY 10016

This edition of *Things I Know About Love* by Kate le Vann,
first published in the United Kingdom in 2006,
is published by arrangement with Piccadilly Press Limited, London, England

1 3 5 7 9 8 6 4 2

www.egmontusa.com

Library of Congress Cataloging-in-Publication Data
Le Vann, Kate.
Things I know about love / Kate Le Vann.
p. cm.
Summary: Seventeen-year-old Livia Stowe travels from England to Princeton,
New Jersey, to visit her brother who is studying there and to celebrate her
recovery from a year-long struggle with leukemia, and while she is there she
writes a blog about her experiences, which include falling in love.
ISBN 978-1-60684-078-8 (hardcover)
[1. British–United States–Fiction. 2. Dating (Social customs)–Fiction.
3. Leukemia–Fiction. 4. Brothers and sisters–Fiction. 5. Blogs–Fiction.
6. Princeton (N.J.)–Fiction.] I. Title.
PZ7.L5722Th 2010
[Fic]–dc22
2009041166

Book design by TME

Printed in the United States of America

CPSIA tracking label information:
Random House Production • 1745 Broadway • New York, NY 10019

things i know about love

July 20

I think this is it: I think I'm going to die. There's this little loose bit on the wing that keeps flapping up and down—is it supposed to do that? The flight attendants are smiling and chatting away with each other . . . they wouldn't do that if the plane was going to crash—would they? Or is that *exactly* what they'd do, because they've been *trained* to, so no one will panic?! Come on, Livia, calm down, no one else looks worried. Wohhohhohh, why is it bumping?! What is doing that? Are we hitting birds? I mean, seriously, are we flying through a flock of emus? Come on, that's *stupid*, Livia. Emus can't fly. Something else big—turkeys. Can turkeys fly? I don't remember anyone ever saying turkeys *can't* fly—if their wingspan . . . Yikes! More bumping! What if the whole plane flips upside down? I hate flying, I hate flying, I hate flying.

I've booted up my computer to write the introduction to my new American Summer blog, because I thought typing would take my mind off the way this plane is bumping like crazy.

The introduction *was* meant to be all important and elegant and meaningful and "This summer marks the voyage of discovery of Livia Stowe," and instead all I'm doing is writing about the plane crashing and when they find my laptop the only message I'll have left for my loved ones and the good of humanity is "Oh, noooooo, we're all going to die! It was the turkeys!"

They *will* know that I knew about the loose bit on the wing.

And didn't tell anyone.

Okay, everything's smoothing out again now. The flap is still flapping, but we've made it through the flying turkeys, and the plane has stopped bumping. The flight attendants still don't seem bothered, so I think maybe I'm not going to die today. In just over two hours, I'll be seeing my brother, Jeff, who is my favorite person in the world. Two hours. I can't believe it. 'Cause he didn't even come home for Christmas last year. Jeff has spent the whole year in Princeton, Noo Joisey. His degree is in American Studies, and that involves spending his third year in America. Studying Americans. Unfortunately for me, he loves it there. To be honest, I'm afraid of how much he loves it: I think he may want to go and live there for good. And then I won't see as much of him. This year has been pretty hard for me. While he was at uni in Manchester, he was only half an hour away, and he came back home all the time, usually with a sack of dirty laundry that contained every single item of clothing he owned. We still hung out and it was really cool, and I didn't mind so much that he'd left home. This year, I've been talking to him mostly by e-mail, with a few bumpy Internet phone calls at midnight, and he sends links to pictures he's put online showing how much fun he's having. Jeff was going to come straight back to see me after term ended last month, but I really didn't want him to. For one thing, he's having the time of his life. For another, I know why Jeff really used to come home so much. It was to see me: he was worried about me and he still is. I've been fine for so long now, and I want us all to forget that I'm the sick little sister who used to look weakly up at him from hospital beds. I'm not her anymore: Leukemia Livia. Brave little Livia. Now I'm flies-halfway-around-the-world-to-see-her-brother-just-because-she-misses-him Livia. Because-she-can Livia. I survived.

Of course it was a nightmare convincing Mum I needed this trip. Yes, *needed*. Not just *could handle*. I turned seventeen this month, July 2, so it shouldn't even *be* up to her whether I fly to America or not. (Well, apart from her paying for the flight. Admittedly, that's a *kind of* important part of it.) But my mum has been through *everything* with me, and has kept me sane while she went nuts. I don't want her hair to turn gray with worry; I don't want to act like I don't understand or don't appreciate her concern for me. Mum is not overprotective as a means of control; she just genuinely believes I'm going to die all the time. And you can sort of get why, because not all that long ago, people were always telling her I might. But my favorite doctor, Dr. Kothari, helped me to make the case. She reminded Mum that I'm taking, like, a tenth as many pills as I used to take when I was fifteen, and by now I am *amazing* at taking pills. Open mouth, insert pill, swallow. (Not like when I started, and Mum had to crush them into powder between two spoons and hide the powder in snack cakes.) Dr. Kothari promised her that every trip to hospital now was becoming more of a formality, and we'd all had to start talking about *EastEnders* more than cell counts because there was nothing new to say. The next checkup wasn't due for a few months, so in the meantime why shouldn't I take a break? Mum wasn't convinced and we went home. But I hadn't given up. As we drove, I pointed out to her that I'd be having checkups for another ten years, at *least*, and I couldn't put my life on hold till I was thirty.

"If it means you'll stay healthy *beyond* thirty, it's not such a bad idea," Mum said.

"Well, what if I *die* at thirty?" I said, which was really insensitive, but I was getting frustrated. "What if I die, and the only other rooms I've ever slept in apart from my bedroom are hospital wards?"

And then my mum started crying and couldn't speak to me, and when we got home, she went and did a big, mad pile of ironing in the kitchen. I felt horrible.

We didn't discuss the matter again for ages, and then a few days before my birthday Jeff's present came—a web camera so we could chat online. We set it up, and suddenly there was Jeff, looking a bit pixilated and jerky, but still unmistakably being Jeff, grinning at us through the computer screen. My mum *loved* it. She made him stand up and show her what he was wearing. She made him take the camera around his room to see how clean it was. Soon, Mum was using Jeffcam more than me, chatting to him late at night—I could hear them both laughing.

We went shopping the following Sunday, and I was looking at some really cute, but quite expensive, blue checked pajamas, just because I really like nightwear, and . . . Oh, blimey, it's because

I spent so much time in hospital, isn't it? Other girls my age lust after sexy boots or something; I get excited by pajamas! Anyway, Mum said she'd buy them for me, and I said, "Come on, you already bought me too much stuff for my birthday. I don't need them."

She said, "Look, we'll put them on your dad's credit card." This is the credit card my dad pays off as part of their divorce agreement, as long as whatever is put on it is important or necessary for me or my brother. He's really good about it—he never complains, even when we sometimes put some *slightly* unnecessary stuff on it. Like my laptop, although I did really need that for doing catch-up coursework when I was in hospital. Like Jeff's PlayStation. "Anyway," Mum said, "you'll want them for Princeton."

Then *I* started crying right in the middle of the shop.

"What do you mean?" I said, because I knew if she didn't say it twice I hadn't heard her properly.

"You should go," Mum said. "Jeff tells me you should. He misses you."

"But I thought . . . You've got to come, too," I said. "Seriously. You'll feel happier about how safe I am, and you miss Jeff as much as I do, and it'll be so much better with you there."

I know other girls my age probably wouldn't think of a holiday with their mum as Fun Central, but I'm weird like that and I really meant it. The truth is, I found it got harder keeping up normal friendships the longer I stayed away from school. When friends came to visit me in hospital, they often didn't know how to talk to me. If they came in groups, they relaxed a bit more and just started talking about school stuff, and that was fun, but it was kind of depressing, too. The stories never had anything to do with me, there were private jokes that "would take too long to explain," and I'm sure they didn't want to keep things from me, but I felt left out a lot. I could just feel myself getting shyer, and I could tell they were starting to think of me as someone different and treating me like I was . . . *strange*, kind of like my personality was in quarantine. It felt all one-way: they talked, they got on with life; I listened and heard about it. Friendships, the way I used to know them, always seemed to be drifting out of reach because I didn't really factor in anyone's plans anymore. My mum was the constant. And the illness took her away from her life, too—she could have gone on more dates, found a new man, seen more of *her* friends . . . but she had to look after me. She never made me feel guilty about it. Really, truly: I worked that out later. Because we had to spend so much time together, we had to become real friends.

We *are* real friends. It goes beyond the parent thing.

In the end, Mum said she couldn't take so much time off work, and she definitely couldn't afford flights for two *and* a hotel, certainly not for more than a week. And I should go for more than a week, and she'd already started making plans with Jeff.

I literally could not believe it.

So if I die on this plane after all that, I'm going to be so pissed off.

I'm determined that this blog will be a total—oh, what's the word—*departure* from my last one, which, to be honest, kind of mutated into a geekalicious episode-and-trivia guide to the 1980s sci-fi TV show *When Voyager*, which I became obsessed with watching on cable TV when I was housebound.

On the other hand, I don't want to do just a straight diary. I want it to have, you know, a *point*. I want to use these observations to help me understand my life. Everyone else I know has been out there getting practical experience, and I'm always behind. I've got all this *theoretical* knowledge: I've seen loads of talk shows and sad films and I must have been through every possible combination of love affairs on telly programs. The challenge is to make theory and real life match up.

So this is going to be about working out love.

It's about the love I have known, and the love I have yet to know. And why, no matter what the world spits at me, I will always chase after that one supreme emotion . . . because, you know, when you feel it, it makes all other things seem a little bit *yeah-yeah, and* . . . ? But that's why this has to be a private blog for the foreseeable future. Because falling in love, even when it's unrequited, is not something that happens to only one person. The other person can't help getting involved—whether they like it or not—and I don't want to embarrass anyone, or hurt anyone, least of all myself. So I've unchecked the box that makes my blog viewable, and although that means I won't be getting any advice from strangers, it also means I won't be getting angry e-mails from people who've spotted themselves on my page.

This summer is about making a fresh start, to reflect my new status as a full adult who will soon have the right to vote. (Ack, the political future of the country at my fingertips—like I needed any more pressure. I don't even know the difference between the Home Secretary and the Foreign Secretary! I mean, clearly one does Home stuff and one does Foreign stuff, but what is the stuff?) So I'm forgiving myself for all my past mistakes, but that doesn't mean that everything that's gone before will now be consigned to the bin bag of time. Ohhh no, everything I've been through is useful in gaining *true* knowledge and understanding of the ways of love. For that reason, this blog will contain actual case studies of my past relationships, in case they throw light on anything yet to come.

Admittedly, there aren't that many.

But that's my **first rule:** I have to dispassionately review all the romantic experiences that have gone wrong (and the bits that went right).

The **second rule** is that I have to have some more experiences, or this blog is going to be pretty boring. I need to move on and take chances when they find me. To be fearless even if it means getting hurt again.

The **third rule** is that I have to tell the truth, even when it makes me look bad. I'm not going to learn anything about love if I skip the parts that make me want to hide behind the sofa. It's amazing how fast your mind blanks out details. I'm going to write everything down as quickly as possible. I know it's going to make me cringe sometimes, but I think it's the only way to do it properly.

Case Study A: Darren

Year nine. I was still thirteen. Saira, who was my best friend at the time—and still is, but in between, I was best mates with Boo, and now there's more like a group of us rather than lots of pairs—told me Darren fancied me. We were in double math, and she was using an incredibly complicated series of clues because she'd been sworn to secrecy by his best friend, Scott Wrexham. "He does not have a black bag. He has never been out with Steph Lindall. He's shorter than Scott Wrexham.

"Well? Are you interested?" Saira demanded.

"I'm not sure I know who it is!"

"It's . . . obviously . . . ," she said, writing **D-A-R-R-E-N** on my notebook at the same time and underlining it. "Come on, what am I going to tell Scott?" She scribbled the name out.

"I don't know," I said. I started scribbling out the name even more darkly until there was a dent in the book. I was terrified because I had never had a boyfriend of any kind. "Don't tell him anything. Please."

"He loves your hair," Saira said.

"My hair?" I said, touching it defensively, without thinking. As a ginger-haired girl, I was well used to people making fun of my hair. I thought this had to be a joke.

"Yeah, seriously. He thinks it's pretty. Well, do you hate him?" Saira asked.

"No, I don't *hate* him," I said. "I've hardly ever spoken to him! I hardly know him!" Although I didn't say it, what I did know about him wasn't 100 percent fanciable. He was a bit of a science nerd. He knew about stuff like tornadoes and lizards.

"Right then, what's the harm? Just give him a go," Saira said.

I didn't want to give him *anything*. I was quite happy without boyfriend trouble. Saira promised not to talk to Scott about me and, although I couldn't meet Darren's eye again for weeks, it all went quiet.

Then we went to Amy Thurgood's Valentine's party. All my friends were dancing, but I was feeling quite tired, so I went to the "chill-out room," which was basically a little dining room separated from the kitchen by hinged frosted-glass doors. With a shock I realized Darren was sitting in there on his own, reading a Terry Pratchett novel. I couldn't just turn around and walk out again, even though I was embarrassed. So I sat down and went through my bag for a bit of lipstick and powder, and said the first thing that came into my head, which was, "That music's loud, isn't it?" Great. Really cool, Grandma.

"Yeah," Darren said. "Not so loud in here, though."

"Right," I said. "It's a bit quieter in here." I asked him about his book. We talked a bit about what had gone on in school that week, and I remember I just got this feeling, all of a sudden, like a crazy feeling, sort of, *This is the moment where your life changes. You're going to have your first kiss now*, and then I realized that for something to happen, I had to get from my side of the room to Darren's side without making a fool of myself. By then, the crazy *This is the moment* feeling was making my heart start pumping like mad.

"You wanna go back in and dance?" Darren asked.

"No, I'm all right here," I said. "What about you?"

"I'm all right here," he said, and for a second it flashed through my head that Saira had got it wrong and he was hoping I'd leave him alone. He sort of slid off his chair and sat on the floor, and I did the same, and we were both sitting on the carpet, with our backs against opposite walls, looking at each other through dining table legs. Sometimes one of us leaned to one side so we could see each other better, and sometimes we leaned at the same time, so the table legs were still in the way, which was quite funny. My heart still wouldn't give it a rest; it kept pumping too much blood into my cheeks. Whenever I put my hand on them, my hand was cold and clammy and my face was hot, which meant *red*. You'll know this if you're ginger—when your face is red, red isn't the word. Your skin is nuclear powered.

I had to get over to Darren's side of the table, but I couldn't think of how to do it. I started threading my fingers through the deep carpet pile. It was the same sort of pattern as our tabby cat.

It was Saira who made the move for both of us. She came in and checked us out and gave me a little knowing look.

"Er, you've got to see this, Liv," she said, waving a padded photograph album. "It's Amy in a ballet outfit. It's classic."

The picture was funny and quite mean, and Darren and I moved close to Saira to look at it and we all laughed. Then Saira said she had to show it to Pritti, too, and off she went. Darren and I were now on the same side of the table. He just leaned in for the kiss; he didn't try to talk his way into it.

I've heard you never forget your first kiss. This is how mine went: Darren moved his tongue in a circle around the inside of my mouth, a move I would later hear friends describe as a "washing machine" but at the time I thought it was how everyone kissed and I didn't know whether I was supposed to do the same to him. A weird thing happened: my heart went from very fast to slow, and it was like all my thoughts were a bag of marbles that had dropped on a wooden floor, shooting out in all directions then slowing down and coming to nothing—a mix of embarrassment and politeness and *boredom*. Suddenly all I could do was think, not feel. *Do I not like kissing?* I remember thinking. *Or do I not like kissing* Darren?

At that moment, Amy's mum came downstairs and we could hear her in the living room telling everyone that the party was ending *now* and we could all call our parents if they weren't already on their way. It turned out someone had brought some beer and Amy's mum, who'd been sitting upstairs watching telly with Amy's dad, had come down for a quick check and found one of the cans. Darren and I had to walk back in to join the rest of the party. I remember we were holding hands, because there didn't really seem to be a choice. Saira was grinning at me and at that precise moment I felt good. Better than good. I was one of the girls who kissed boys now. I was on the team. He asked me for my e-mail address, and I wrote it on the inside of a cupcake wrapper and stuffed it into his hand as we went out to Saira's dad's car. By the time I got home, Darren had already sent me an e-mail asking if we could go out, and I e-mailed back to say I would really like that.

For our first date we went to see a film on Saturday afternoon. When the lights went out totally and the film started, he took hold of my hand, and we held hands with our fingers locked, and I realized my hand was getting really sweaty. I unlocked my fingers, just *slid* the hand out, and pretended I was doing my hair but really I was trying to wipe the hand-sweat off. Then he wanted to hold my hand *again*, and I was thinking, *For God's sake*, why? *Can you not feel the hand-sweat? Do you think it's normal that* you and I *are making this much hand-sweat together?* We didn't go any further in the cinema. Afterwards, he took me to a café that only served potatoes. So we ate potatoes—you know, with fillings—and talked about the film, and I realized that I'd made a terrible mistake. I didn't fancy Darren and I knew I didn't want to snog him again. But I didn't know how the date was going to end and how I'd get away. While we were walking back towards the town center, I saw my bus was coming up to a nearby stop, and I said, "Listen the film went on longer than I thought I've *really* got to get home oh there's my bus bye!" and just legged it. Later, I e-mailed him this:

Hi Darren. Thanks for the film. And the spud! Listen, I'm not really that into going out with people at the moment. I've got loads of work to do for my flute exam and I just don't think I'm going to have the time to go out that much. I had a really nice time today, but I think we probably shouldn't go out with each other.

Thanks a lot. L x

"And the spud!" Yeah, that's cool, Livia. He e-mailed me back: *Have I done something wrong?*

Me: *No, of course not! Am just really busy.*

Him: *Can we just meet up tomorrow? I'd really like another chance to talk to you.*

Me: *Well, I just don't think there's any point, you know? It's really stupid, but I really am swamped with work and have to practice my flute and stuff.*

I still have the e-mails: I'm cutting and pasting from my old Hotmail account. And even though I've promised to tell the whole truth and nothing but the truth, I think the e-mail reporting can stop there, because it didn't get any better. Basically, I didn't realize how angry Darren was going to be and was too stupid to predict what would happen. The next week at school, by the time I got in, everyone was laughing at me and calling me frigid–Jeez, I was still *thirteen*!–because I'd only kissed Darren once, "on the cheek." He said it was on the cheek, but when he'd kissed me it was definitely *not* on the cheek. There was tongue, there was washing-machine action, and there was the unmistakable taste of smoky bacon crisps. But I'd been knocked flat by this, well, teasing *is* the word, but it feels more like assassination. Boys I hated were quoting bits of my e-mail at me, and pretending to ask me out and then saying, "I know your flute is very important to you, but you can practice on *my* flute anytime," and then laughing, doing like, you know, dirty jokes. I just wanted to leave school and never come back.

Later, you wonder how it is that he's the one being rejected and you're the one being laughed at. It's a clever trick–I wish I could do it. Anyway, let's see what we've learned.

Things I know about love.

1. Nothing that happens between two people is guaranteed to be private.

July 21

It's about–gah, the math is difficult because my laptop is still on British time–five a.m., and, naturally, I can't sleep. It's 10:13 a.m. at home. I'm starving. But I can hardly bounce into my brother's room, wake him up, and ask him to point me towards the Frosties.

Who cares? I'm here! In the United States of America! Jeff was at the airport waiting for me, holding up a jokey little sign that said *STOWE* on it, like one of the airport chauffeurs. Then we had about an hour's drive from the airport–he'd borrowed a car from a friend; loads of American students have cars–and everything just looked so *American*. We went past shops with neon signs saying DRUGSTORE and LIQUOR STORE, and the traffic lights dangled from cables, and, of course, we were driving on the wrong side of the road. We turned off the main motorway and started to head towards Jeff's flat, when a giant sandy-colored dog ran across the road, right in front of us. I screamed and Jeff banged on the brakes. He said it was actually a small deer, that they sometimes did that, but they hardly ever got hit.

When you leave the big roads, which are lined with scary giant warehouse-type shops, it's like a little old-fashioned village: the houses are made of wood and painted pastel colors, with porches. There are quite a few fairy lights on the outside of people's houses, even though it's nowhere near Christmas. Loads of the gardens have *really* big American flags on poles, or flags hanging from the roof. That's pretty weird. Imagine going through normal residential streets in Liverpool and seeing great big Union Jacks waving in the gardens. Jeff's professor's flat doesn't have a flag. Jeff is housesitting for the summer—his professor is doing research in Mexico and didn't want to leave the flat empty. And this means I get to stay here with him—there'd have been no chance of me squeezing into Jeff's old dorm room; I'd have had to stay in a hotel, which would have been too expensive . . . and lonely. The house is small. I would have thought a Princeton professor would have a bigger place. Other people's homes always make me uncomfortable at first, as if someone else can hear everything you're saying but you can't see them—as if they've left part of themselves there to spy on you. That is, now that I write it down, nuts. There are two bedrooms, but mine looks more like a study—there are so many history books. There are even history books in the bathroom.

The hunger is now *painful*. Last night, when I got in, Jeff tried to make me eat dinner, but not only had I eaten a heavy, greasy plane meal with all the extras and most of the giant chocolate bar I'd taken on board, but it was also about two a.m. British time. I was *sooo* tired and, no matter how much I love and missed Jeff, I just wanted to sleep. But he was all bouncy and enthusiastic and took me out to a little Chinese restaurant, where I drank a whole pot of tea and stared at the food as if it were made of plastic. Now, I want to eat everything I didn't eat last night.

Just sneaked out to the kitchen and there were some doughnuts from yesterday. Sorry, *donuts*. So I'm eating one of those, and it tastes absolutely delicious. Full-fat, full-sugar American delicious. Wow, I'm really here.

July 22

Back in England, I had a little going-away party before I set off. It was just a few girls–Hannah, Steph, Boo, and Saira–and we ordered in pizza and stayed up talking well into the night. Boo, Hannah, and Steph are going to university at the end of September. Saira's taking a year off in Australia. Her cousin lives there, but she's going to go all over it and maybe "hop across" to Japan. Nearer the end of summer, the uni-bound girls are going on a little holiday together somewhere closer, like Spain. I didn't talk too much about my plans–and the thing is, everyone was so excited about this, America, the adventure I'm on now, so that's what we talked about. I just can't think further ahead until I know what my final exam results are. I missed so much of the last year that I'm the only one of us who didn't apply to university, the only one without a plan–but the same fear of the future was everyone's unspoken thought all evening: what happens to us now, and will we stay in touch? Everyone moves around so much these days, and it's supposed to have made the world smaller—even so, one of our closest and sweetest friends, Chloe, left school at sixteen and went to work in Leeds. We see her at Christmas, but I've been finding it harder to know what to write in e-mails to her. So much happens to her between the e-mails that you have to go back and read the previous ones to remember who's who.

And here's my brother, miles and miles farther from home than I ever knew he could be, and before I came out here to see him, I spent so much time worrying that becoming grown-ups meant growing apart. This summer, it's like this is the closest to real, proper friends we've ever been, but I'm afraid of it being the closest we'll ever be . . . and of there being less in the future.

Then there's my dad. At the time of the divorce, he promised nothing would change and we'd always be his kids and he'd always love us and come and see us all the time. But his work took him to the other side of the country, and his weekends started getting busier. I know Mum sometimes used his credit card to punish him for letting us down . . . or maybe it really was to cheer us up. Either way, I didn't want to punish him and I didn't want to be compensated. I just wanted a little more time with him. When we talk now, we both know we've lost something, and I can feel us trying to fake it and make up what's missing. The faking makes me sad, and the sadness makes the faking harder to do.

This is making me feel quite weepy about Mum. I'm missing her. Since Jeff left, she and I have developed little routines—just, you know, the way we eat breakfast together, the way we watch *Coronation Street*, the pizzas we make from scratch on Saturdays. This morning, when I had breakfast with Jeff, I thought about

Mum on her own, putting toast in only one side of the toaster because we always have one slice each, reading the paper but having no one to read out stories to.

Okay, had a little cry. Back now.

Part of me is *so desperate* for new things to happen, new experiences, and to grow as a person now. And part of me knows that there's *nothing* to stop me from doing any of that but that I stand to lose so much when I do. This is the first time I've been away from home, and Jeff is here! So *home* is here! But I'm scared and sad because my mum is not.

And it's *so* insane because I had a fab day today. Jeff and I walked around Princeton and ate ice cream from a little shop in a pretty, old-fashioned square. He told me about this girl he's completely obsessed with, Krystina. Her family lives in the town and she's a student here.

"The thing is," Jeff said, "I have no way of working out whether she fancies me."

"Does *she* get in touch with you or is it the other way around?"

"She always calls me and asks me to parties. But when I go, nothing happens between us. She doesn't want to hang out at the end of the night with me, she never gets any closer, and I seem to have been stuck in the same place with her forever. So I think that means we're just friends."

"Have you . . . made a move?" I said. I couldn't believe I was talking to Jeff like this. Jeff never talked about his personal life before. I felt so close to him, and on his level in a different way.

"Well . . . how do you mean?" Jeff said. "I haven't, you know, *made* a *move* made a move, but she must know how I feel."

"Like you know how she feels?"

"Yeah, I see what you're saying," Jeff said. "But girls know, don't they? Girls always know what everyone's thinking–that's what makes them so cool."

I wonder if that's really what all boys think about all girls, or if Jeff and I are just equally useless at love. I never know what anyone's thinking.

After our ice cream, we ducked out of the sunshine so Jeff could show me where he did his work. Well, that's what he said, but I think he was hoping to spot this Krystina, although he didn't find her. Most of the students had left for summer vacation, and those still scattered around tended to be the older graduate students, but the ones I saw were just the most amazing physical specimens of male studenthood. Tanned skin, broad shoulders, lush hair. You just think: *Well, they all drank up their milk when they were kids, didn't they?* The girls all wear denim minis and have long brown legs stretching for miles down into little flat sneakers, and I did feel small and sickly and weedy around them. On the other hand, they actually didn't look as sexy as the girls at my school do. They were quite *safe*. Too many pastel shades. Where I'm from, you get packs of girls who are really wild looking, and properly drop-dead sexy, too. I've always been too scared to make eye contact in case they beat me up, but I can't help peeking because I want to learn how they manage to look pretty and edgy like that. Here in Princeton, the girls don't look like they could terrify the boys. So maybe these perfect students still have a thing or two to learn.

Ha, like I can talk! Look at me: black T-shirt and cut-off jeans. Oh, yeah, really fierce, Livia.

When we were having lunch in the student cafeteria, an English boy called Adam, who's a friend of Jeff's, came up and said hi. He said he'd met *me* before, when I came to see Jeff at Manchester—he's at university there, too. I did meet a lot of Jeff's friends when I went to visit, but there were so many, and I was really shy and kept my head down, *plus,* I was very depressed at the time, for reasons that I have to cover in a Case Study. I didn't remember Adam today, anyway, but I panicked and pretended I did.

"Oh, yeah," I said. "You were at that . . . forgotten the name of the *place* now. But of course I remember you."

Adam's eyes narrowed just a tiny amount, and his mouth curved into a one-sided smile.

"Fibber," he said.

I was so embarrassed that I laughed out loud, a kind of gasping, single-"ha" laugh.

"Yes," I said, trying to make my mind up about whether to lie again. "Yes, I do remember."

He smirked a little bit more, but this time his mouth relaxed into a wide, lovely grin.

"You so do not," he said. "Fine, I'm going to give you a multiple choice. Did we talk about nanobots, Johnny Depp, or makeup?"

"Nanobots. Of course," I said, thinking that if I was going to bluff, I might as well sound confident, and there was no way I'd have talked about Johnny Depp, and obviously makeup was out of the ques– Ohh! And *now* I remembered him. We'd talked about makeup. *"No!"* I shouted, interrupting what he was about to say. "You gave me a tissue," I added softly. I'd been visiting my brother in his first year, when I was fifteen and had felt a bit overwhelmed seeing him in the student surroundings. It all seemed very far away from his life with me back home, quite dangerous and unprotected. I'd popped out to get chewing gum—that was my excuse—and believed I'd got away with a secret little blub in the street because the situation felt too big for me. But I didn't realize that I was heading back in with two thick black lines of cried-through mascara down my cheeks. Adam had been heading out the door I was heading through, and asked if I was okay. I had said, "Of course, why wouldn't I be?" and he pointed at his cheeks briefly, then held up a shiny metal key ring that acted like a mirror, so I could see my black-streaked face. He gave me a tissue and assured me it was clean, and I gabbled on for a minute about the problems with wearing mascara, then we both went on in our different directions.

Adam studies computing and has been in Manchester all year, but is spending the summer in Princeton with his older brother, Dougie, who studies here full-time and is apparently some kind of computer genius. They've been working on a programming project together, although when he started to explain it my mind went all spacey, and I had to stop myself from saying, "How can someone be as into computers as you are and be so cute?" He has longish, dark brown hair that goes just a bit flicky over his ears, and brown eyes, with black eyelashes that make them seem darker, and he is the perfect shape, like a lean, upside-down triangle. He was wearing good clothes too, just a gray T-shirt with some darker gray squiggles on it and faded gray jeans, but, you know, the perfect shape for both T-shirts and jeans. I don't know why I'm talking about shapes so much. Anyway, shape-wise, Adam is doing all right. In my experience, a lot of the boys who are real computer-heads tend to be pale-skinned sci-fi fans. Not that there's anything wrong with that—I happen to be a pale-skinned sci-fi fan myself—but that doesn't mean I have to *fancy* other see-through geeks. So let's hope Adam isn't as picky as me.

I told him about the blog I'd started, but I stopped short of telling him its higher purpose—the "working out love" part—because I knew it would sound mad.

"So where can I read it?" he said.

"It's locked. I mean, it's private," I said. "I don't want to . . . it's really more like a diary."

"But I thought the point of blogs was that they were public?"

"Well, using a blog site means that I can add to it from anywhere, and I don't always have my own computer with me. It's safer, too—it means no backing up. I do like reading other people's blogs, but I'm not ready to have them read mine—that's not why I'm writing it."

"Why *are* you writing it?"

"Have you never kept a diary?" I asked him.

"No."

I shrugged. "Maybe you should try it."

"Why, though?" Adam asked. "I always hated writing the "How I Spent My Summer Holidays" essay at school, and now you're telling me I should do that for fun?"

"Well, you get to know yourself better. You write about events when they happen to you, but then later you can read what you said about them, and enough time has passed for you to not remember *exactly* how you were feeling at the time, and you can see where you've gone wrong, or right. It's always surprising—your attitude always changes. Maybe it was a huge deal at the time and now you have no idea why it upset you. Sometimes you forget little details, really lovely things, and when you're reminded, it's . . ." I was somewhere between feeling tingly-happy and being embarrassed about my enthusiasm, because the fact is I *love diaries*—I reread and treasure all of mine, even though they make me cringe sometimes. "Sorry, I feel a bit silly now. I suppose I just like the fact that there are books where I'm the main character," I finally said, with a smile, worried about coming across as a weirdo. "I'm obviously really conceited."

"I don't think that's true," Adam said. He was smiling, too, but not at my "joke"—the smile was softer, and his gaze held mine until I could feel myself starting to blush. Stupid ginger-hair skin. You only have to slightly have an emotion, like barely more than being conscious, and your cheeks tell the room what it is. "And what are you going to write about today?"

"Well, I'm not sure. Nothing really happened today. I'm still a bit jet—"

"'Talked to an incredibly boring English bloke. Cannot believe I've come halfway round the world and I'm stuck with one of my brother's mates from Manchester. . . .' That sort of thing?"

"No!" I giggled.

"You know what I'd like you to put?"

"What?" I asked, and I actually *shivered*.

"Ran into a boy called Adam again. . . ." He stopped, and enough silence passed that I worried about filling it. When he started again, his tone had changed; it was lighter but more distant. "Yeah, it's harder than it looks, isn't it? I should really leave it to you, I think."

So: *I ran into a boy called Adam again. And* . . .
He's right, this is harder than it looks.

blogplace: Inside Adam—*good title, eh?*

JULY 22

THERE IS no getting past this: diaries are for girls. Girls love diaries. My sister used to get one every year for Christmas and kept it hidden under the big pink furry elephant on top of her wardrobe (Colonel Trumpety). And even then the diary had an actual lock and key. She was not, as far as I know, working as a spy for the British government. These were, in my opinion, excessive security measures.

I say that, but while I was setting up this blog, I used a fake address and checked five times that I'd set it so it wasn't open to the public—the same as Livia's. Did a search for it. It's all safe. Not a trace. Obviously did a search for hers, too. Obviously didn't find it.

Livia is Jeff Stowe's sister, and I met her again today, and because of that, I—if you can believe it—am trying to write a blog. Just because I'm bored and we talked about blogs. And maybe because I think a part of me is hoping she'll crack my code and find it and discover that I've fallen for her as quickly as I did the first time I met her when I bumped into her in Manchester and she'd been crying and I just . . . You know how there are some girls you just want to hold and be held by? I should have asked her out or something today, just casually, like, "I'm a Brit, you're a Brit, shall we go and laugh at Americans together?" Instead, I just asked her a bunch of boring questions and talked too much about myself, and now I'm thinking about her way too much, and I've come back and set up a blog. Stop being a nutter, Adam.

I think I should ask her out, but she's a mate's sister, so I'm not sure. My brother says why not ask her to the semi-party he's having the day after tomorrow. Or, in Dougie's own words, "Why are you being such a fairy about this? Just ask her." But Dougie's mates will be there, I don't know if it'd be her scene—they'll probably start watching *Star Wars* movies, and I think making a girl watch sci-fi on a first "date" is roughly equivalent to wearing a T-shirt that says, BY THE WAY, I DON'T REALLY BELIEVE IN PERSONAL HYGIENE.

According to Livia, when I read what I've just written now in the future, it's going to make me understand myself better. Unfortunately, I think I understand myself too well already. And diaries are for girls.

July 23

I need to fill in a bit of backstory before I go on. I'll be as brief as I can be, I promise. But my life is still all wrapped up in this, and I . . . I had a really tough time. It upsets me to write about it and I want to write my valuable love analysis, not sit and cry about that time, and it's making me teary already—it always does. I just still can't talk about it easily, even though I know that makes me seem like I feel sorry for myself too much. I was diagnosed with leukemia just before I turned fourteen—I actually thought I'd caught mono from Darren. I got a sore throat soon after snogging him, and at the time he had some kind of cough. He was clearing his throat a lot. Stupidly, I thought this was proof that I'd snogged him properly and not on the cheek! I used to daydream about getting up in front of class and shouting in my new hoarse voice, "Hey, everyone! Listen to this! *Scraaaar.* [That's the sound of me inhaling at the time.] I only kissed him on the cheek, did I? So how come I've got this cold, too? *Scraaaar.*" I'm not a *"Scraaaar"*-out-loud sort of girl, though: I just burned with silent rage and shot him stink-eye looks.

In the meantime, the cold wouldn't go away. Every morning I woke up and the first thing I thought about was how my throat was really sore, and after *weeks* of this, I saw the doctor and . . . When they tell you, you're just like, *Oh, leukemia, I've read about that, I'm dead now, that's bad.* The worst bit was coming out of the doctor's office to find my mum to bring her back into the office with me. She was casually reading a prehistoric copy of *Hello* magazine ("Henry VIII tells all about his breakup with Anne"), waiting patiently the way she always did when she came with me to the doctor's. She knew straightaway that something was wrong. Just from the look on my face. When I said we couldn't go home yet she said, "What's wrong?" really loudly, kind of getting on for hysterical already, and people looked at us.

They put me on steroids first. Steroids can make you fat. They made me fat. I know I'd just been diagnosed with cancer and had more important things to worry about, and I had fatter friends who were sexy and pretty, and I would have swapped places with them in a heartbeat. But still, there's something about getting fat when it's beyond your control that just feels . . . like the last straw—one more piece of bad luck that's almost funny, but almost enough to make you give up. You have cancer, and you're buying size 16 jeans when four months ago you were buying size 8 jeans, and isn't cancer supposed to make you waste away, anyway? I didn't need any more ways of feeling worse.

Every time I had another doctor's appointment, my mum and I would go into the office and we'd tell each other—and we'd both really believe it because we wanted it so much—that this time the doctor would say everything had worked and we could start smiling again, could both start living again. But instead, every time, the doctor's voice got quiet and the news was bad again. We'd walk out in silence, and I'd be trying not to cry, for my mum, but the tears would just fall out of my eyes anyway, as if the normal muscles that used to be able to hold them back had broken.

At this point, part of me wished I could just get it over with and die, because I was sick of putting my family through it. I thought if I died they'd get a break from always having to worry about me and always having to be around to hear worse news. It felt like I was failing them when the treatments didn't work. *They* were all doing everything they could, being supportive, buying me presents, keeping me smiling, and just waiting for me to do my part, which was: get better. I couldn't even do that for them. I sometimes fantasized about the doctor saying, "Listen, we're all *very* sorry about this, but we've tried and it's too much; it just can't be cured." At least, I'd have been able to let go. You always read about people *beating* their illnesses—it's never supposed to be luck. If you're not getting over yours, obviously it's your fault, you're just not trying hard enough.

But how do you try?

You look at your body and there are parts of it you can't touch or control or even see, and you *think* at them—you just *think*; that's all you have—"Come on, pull yourself together, cells, let's fight this disease."

Nothing happens.

It's not like you can do exercise. Or diet, or eat more. Or

study. You can't *do* anything, but that doesn't make it any easier. It's not just the side effects of the drugs and the pain of the illness and the tiredness—the hardest part is being brave so that nobody knows that you are sad *all the time*. They know you're sad sometimes, and they can cope with helping you through those times. But if my mum had known how much I was sad, and how exhausted I was, and how much I wanted to cry every minute of every day, she would not have been able to cope. Being brave is not a part of your personality, it's your job. It's what you owe the people who love you.

So I didn't tell my mum everything. I didn't tell her about the loneliness of the hospital at night, and how I used to be afraid that random crazy people would run in and kill me. Or that I'd hear the squeak of the nurse's rubber-soled shoes, or the creak of her cart, and wish she'd come in and talk to me, but I was too shy to bother her. And I'd wake up every morning at five a.m. and just wish and wish and wish for hours that my mum would get there quickly and say hi, and as soon as she got there everything was better, but the countdown to her leaving had already begun.

Okay, seriously, let's hurry back to the love part. *Obviously* they found something that fixed me, and it was nothing to do with me getting braver, or fighting harder, or being stronger. Just luck. Just amazingly good luck. I notice stories about other sick teenagers more than most people my age do, and I know that when they don't get better, it's not because they were lazier than me, or weaker. So I feel guilty, sometimes, about living, and hope I can be worthy of it and make my life worth the second chance I've been given. I don't feel like I can take it for granted.

32

At sixteen, I'd made it through bone-marrow transplants, and was only having to go for checkups every couple of weeks. I was getting thinner, but I was still a lot fatter than I had been before I'd started to get sick. I was terrified of being seen again by people who hadn't seen me for ages. I'd been out of school for well over a year and hadn't socialized in all that time. I felt like a freak—*was* a freak.

But it's funny, when you're separated from all school life, you develop a strange kind of confidence at the same time. For one thing, you're literally dealing with life-and-death issues about yourself, so you stop worrying about small things you once obsessed over—for me, things like whether my nose bent slightly to the right, or whether the muscles next to my knees were freakishly big. You stop asking "Does my bum look big in this?" after you've gained more than thirty pounds and lost most of it again and you realize how thin you used to be when you used to think you were fat. It goes beyond all of that, even: in hospital, everything happens in a kind of time-has-stopped, not-real world, where people feel sorry for you and the people you meet are all kind and lovely and tell you how pretty and young you are. This is so different from school, which is a kind of scary jungle where anyone could be out to get you any day just because they feel like it, and you don't feel young or pretty, and you have to watch your back all the time. When you go straight from one place to the other, the weird artificial confidence bursts like a bubble-gum bubble all over your face. You know the other kids know all about you, and that they know they're supposed to be nice to you, but, what with you being a freak and all, it's not going to be easy for them. . . .

Case Study B: *Luke*

When I came back to school, I found out that my friends now ran the place. Around the time I'd left to go into hospital, everyone I knew had been about as cool as I was, i.e., not cool at all. I returned to find myself in some kind of nightclub world where people lazed around on common-room furniture, wearing their own clothes, playing loud music, talking about sex—but in broad daylight. Sixth Form. See, once again, this makes me sound like a mad old lady: school students up to *this* sort of thing? In *broad daylight*? I must write to the *Times*!

Not only was I unprepared for everyone suddenly being as confident as . . . like, C-list celebrities, but there were all these new faces among them. Our school is one of only a few in a fairly big area and, at this stage, the local schools split up and mix a lot. Some people come to our school from other schools, people from our school leave to go to university-prep schools—it depends on the sort of subjects you want to study. Most of the university-prep schools are much more focused, with introductions to subjects like law and psychology. Our school is quite old fashioned and well rounded, but it's also seen as the solid, reliable choice.

I didn't start right at the beginning of the year, so I kind of felt like the new girl for a few weeks, although obviously my friends were there and they were protective of me. I hoped there hadn't been big public announcements about, you know, Leukemia Girl's return, but at the same time I didn't want to have to do any explaining to anyone about my condition, or why I was starting term late. I just wanted to slot in quietly and not be looked at. I wasn't dressed quite like everyone else, because you really have to be around other teenagers to know how everyone's dressing, and you have to think about it every day, which I hadn't been. My clothes were new and I'd loved them when I bought them—I went on a few big shopping trips with my mum especially for that purpose—but they weren't quite right. My skirts were a bit too long, my shoes were too straight—everything was too schooly. I guess all my friends had been going shopping together a lot. There was a *look* now—not just fashion, something more like a uniform but *nothing* like school uniform, and none of my clothes fitted it.

So I was different in lots of ways and, to start with, obsessed with the idea that people were looking at me and talking about me. Gradually, I realized that not only was that not happening, but that I was going *completely* unnoticed most of the time, and that made me feel lonely, and marooned, and out of place. People I'd known quite well before, but wasn't all that close to, were nice and asked how I was, but didn't ask much more. To begin with, I didn't seem to speak at all to people I didn't know, and I didn't expect them to talk to me.

And then, one did: Luke.

"Hey, Red! When's the *Wuthering Heights* essay got to be in by?"

A dark-haired boy, in a green T-shirt with a picture of Elvis on it, was looking straight at me when he called this out. But I didn't think it was me he was asking, so I just frowned at him with this idiotic confusion on my face.

"You're in Gresham's English class, aren't you?" he asked—definitely me this time. "Hello? Do you . . . speak?" he asked sort of mock-innocently, but his dark eyes were shiny and glinting.

"Uh . . . yeah," I said, blinking through my fringe at him. "I . . . didn't think you were talking to me."

"You're in English with me, aren't you? Weren't you the one at the front on the right squeaking about Heathcliff?"

I cleared my throat, so my voice would come out non-squeakily. But then, I just couldn't think of anything to say. He was being so *rude* and he didn't even know me! I was on my own and couldn't start talking to anyone else. I felt fragile, as if my just-mended body would start coming apart at the seams if anyone rattled me.

"The essay has to be in by next Monday," I said politely, and started getting my bag and books together to go. He came over and sat down on the chair next to mine, and put his hand on my knee. Er . . .

"All right, Red," he said. "You don't have to be so chilly. I was just saying hello."

"Well . . . you said I squeaked," I said, looking at his hand and wondering if I should move it, or shake my leg free. I was trying to make it sound like a flirty telling-off, but it didn't come out that way.

"Well, you said I squeaked!" he squeaked loudly, and then laughed just as loudly. God, he was being so nasty! But I just stared at him again, breathing fast through my mouth.

Anyway, that's when I started falling for Luke.

Yeah, I know, it's *nuts*, isn't it? Someone bullies me and I go for it. But Luke had an advantage over the boys I'd grown up with. To him, I wasn't that girl who got leukemia and spent all that time in hospital; I was a stranger with red hair and a mysterious past, and he'd noticed me just because he liked the way I looked. When it came to my old friends, I was desperate to show them that I hadn't changed, and that they didn't need to treat me differently. I wanted them to know I was normal and the same because I didn't want to be damaged. Luke didn't know anything about the "normal" me, which meant that the side of me that had always wanted to be more spontaneous and funnier, and maybe a bit looser, could come out. He seemed to want to drag it out, and that was really why I'd fallen for him. Everyone else was so careful with me, from the people in the hospital, to my family, to my friends. Luke teased me, but he was also goofy and hilarious, and I *needed* that so much. I needed someone to be silly and a bit more rough-and-tumble with me, someone who wouldn't keep stopping to check that I wasn't about to die. Someone who'd grab my hand and run, and keep running—do you know what I mean? For the first time since I'd been old enough to worry about everything, *I* was acting goofy and stupid and giggly. Like for instance, I introduced him to my teddy bears—I mean, can you believe it? I even used to shove them in the wardrobe when my cool girl friends came round. Luke gave the teddies comedy voices that talked to me. ("Helloooo, Liviaaaa, it's Big Furrrry Ted heeeere.")

A really big thing was that, physically, I'd never felt this relaxed with someone else close to me. But Luke just held on to me without even seeming to notice how awkward I was, hugged me all the time, touched my knees when he was talking to me the way he had that first time we spoke. I found myself starting to drape my arm around his shoulders; I gently messed up his hair when I made fun of him. It was spontaneous and easy, but it was still something I noticed myself doing, and loved doing.

Oh, by the way, did I mention the snogging?

Okay, yeah, it turned out it *was* just Darren I didn't like snogging.

Luke and I started looking a lot like boyfriend and girlfriend quite quickly. We hung out after school and went to parties together, or to the bowling alley with other couples, giving ourselves the comedy couple name "Lenny and Penny" on the TV scoreboards. When you've got a real boyfriend, everything stupid is okay, and everything scary feels safe. They do the talking when you don't feel up to it. You can talk about them to other people when you've got nothing else to say, or repeat things they said and pretend you thought of them.

I'd told him, of course. About my illness. Well, some of it, little bits. Luke didn't seem to mind.

"You're okay now, aren't you?" he said, tilting his head on one side and knotting his lovely dark eyebrows with concern. He had these deep, dark eyes that seemed to understand me. We were sitting on swings in the park, even though there was a metal sign screwed to the top of the frame saying no one over twelve could use them. The sun was setting behind a row of houses, and the warm, fading rays made his skin glow. We'd both twisted our swings round and round—something I'd started when I was getting nervous talking about the illness and he'd copied. Now we were facing each other, keeping the chains still by planting our feet in the sand.

"I'm fine now," I said. "Everything's okay now."

"Good," Luke said, and leaned over to touch my cheek with the side of his thumb, then leaned farther, softly kissing my forehead, then, even more gently, my lips. Then we both let our swings unwind, and as they got faster, I started giggling until the swing jerked to a hiccuppy stop. I was dizzy in all sorts of ways and I knew I loved him.

I didn't tell Luke, though, even though he was always telling me he loved me. I didn't know if he meant that, or even wanted me to believe it—he said it too easily. I'd read that if you came on too strong, it put boys off, and I didn't want to do anything to put him off. I don't know if I did anything wrong.

My friends tell me he's just an idiot. I mean, Boo is always sweet about everyone, and she says maybe he just panicked, and it's a big thing for anyone to cope with. Saira is always angry when any of us are hurt, and she's angriest at Luke, saying he's an immature little boy. But I know that all my friends also found it hard to be normal around me when I was ill.

What happened with Luke was that I had to go back into hospital for a week to take drugs through an IV drip—my doctors thought I was having a relapse. I was actually fine—it was just a minor glitch. Luke didn't come to visit me. He sent a card with Hannah and Boo in which he said he couldn't stand hospitals because his granddad had died in one a few years before, and the smell and the color of the walls freaked him out. I was fine with that, although I felt really stupid opening it and having to read it in front of Hannah and Boo. How embarrassing is that, when your boyfriend just sends you a card via your friends, and won't even come to see you? When I came out again, I had to spend a couple of weeks mostly in bed, and he always had an excuse not to come round then, either. I was hurt at first, and then I started to get mad—too mad to make the first move when I was back to normal and should have called him. For a long time afterwards I regretted not calling and blamed myself. If only I'd done it straightaway, before it was too late, and asked him if anything was wrong, then maybe everything would have been okay. If only I'd not sulked, I kept thinking, I'd obviously made the relapse look more serious than it was. Or maybe he was just frightened of not being sensitive enough, or of hurting me, or something like that. Maybe I just left it too late, and things changed too much for us to get back to where we were. As time went on, though, and with input from friends (especially Saira), I came to realize that it hadn't really been up to me to chase after him. It had been Luke's choice not to stay with me.

He'd been texting me while I was recuperating at home, talking about how much work he had to do—texts that reminded me, unfortunately, of my famous "flute practice" e-mail to Darren—and finally, I sent him a text saying: SO WHEN AM I GOING TO SEE YOU?

And waited.

Afterwards, my friends talked quite a lot about how selfish Luke had been. Which is fair enough—I'm sure he is selfish. I'm sure he could have ended things better and been nicer about it. But it doesn't change the facts. He didn't want to go out with me anymore, for *whatever* reason. I assume it was because I got ill again and he didn't like that—that seems the most obvious explanation. But maybe it had been bubbling for a while and I hadn't noticed and this seemed like the sensible moment to break up with me, while we were already apart? Who knows for sure? You can't force someone to fancy you, can you?

Not knowing why is the hardest part. Of course I worry that

there are no boys out there who'll ever really be able to cope with my background, and I worry that I'm damaged goods. I worry boys will never think of me as uncomplicated, pretty, even sexy(!), and only as someone who was ill, no matter how healthy I am, and how long ago it all was. You know, they'll just find out and it'll be, "No, too much trouble," and turn right around and keep going. I worry about that all the time. I hate being different, I hate having to explain and carry around all this extra stuff. I think you can't blame the boys—that's just how they react, and there's no point in Saira getting angry about it. Because, let me confess something horrible, something I'd never tell anyone out loud: I've met boys my age in hospital with leukemia, talked to them a bit, bonded in a way that no one who hasn't been ill like this can ever understand. They can be gorgeous, exactly my type—funny, strong, whatever. And what I think about them is, *Ooh, I don't know—leukemia. Too much trouble.*

So it may or may not be my fault, but it is my problem.

Luke's last text came a full day later, which I suppose doesn't sound very long, but I had checked my phone about six hundred times by then, so it felt like a long time. I just stared at the phone the whole day, basically. I was so happy and my heart stopped for a second when the little envelope appeared on the screen. It said, SORRY MAY AS WELL BE HONEST. LOOK I'D BEEN THINKING BEFORE ALL THIS STUFF HAPPENED THAT WE'D GOT A BIT SERIOUS BEFORE WE WERE READY. LET'S USE THIS BREAK AND TAKE A TIME-OUT, SEE HOW WE FEEL. SORRY, RED. L.

I was too mortified to demand explanations or ask him to give me another chance. I felt physically sick with embarrassment, and weak, as if I were made of paper and could be scrunched up and thrown away. I wanted to hide my face when I went to school—had he asked all his mates for advice, and they'd told him I wasn't worth it? How many people had he discussed us with, and what did they know? Were they all talking about why it was a good idea to ditch me? I didn't try to see him alone again after his text. I was too proud to show him how hurt I was. I saw him at school, and we talked like normal people to each other, except I didn't know when to look at his face, or how *long* to look at his face. When our eyes made contact it was like being slapped, I just wanted to recoil. If we were in a group, or in English class, and he was the person talking, I used to make myself count to three and look at his face for the whole three. If he looked at me, I still had to hold the look, and then I'd look away. But that was hard, and mostly I just couldn't look at him.

What I hated the most was his apologies, when they came, like he knew how much he'd upset me and it was all one-way. It meant he hadn't really liked me at all, because he wasn't sad, and I'd been really into him, because I was. I cried a lot—big surprise. My mum was just matter-of-factly nice to me; she said all the right things, but I don't think she understood how devastated I was. I think my mum thinks anything that happens to me, short of death now, is really quite good luck on balance. Oh, the hairdresser dyed your hair pink? Never mind, love, have some chocolate, you can give it a good brush in the morning and it'll look fine. The love of your life couldn't cope with you being ill and maybe you'll never love or be loved again? Oh, it could be worse, Livi. You know you cry very easily. . . .

Things I know about love.

1. Nothing that happens between two people
is guaranteed to be private.

2. People don't always tell you the truth about how they feel.
And the truth is, it may not be the same as how you feel.

3. I don't know if you ever get over having your heart
broken.

July 25

I've met Krystina, the girl Jeff's so obsessed with. She's amazingly good looking, like a younger Gwyneth Paltrow—that perfect, healthy, American girl look. She has a fat plait of shiny blond hair that sits on one shoulder, her skin is honey-colored and *glows*, and her teeth are like a toothpaste ad. Ha, what am I, Jeff's diary? But, oh yeah, I can see why he's so love-struck.

I really hope she isn't out of his league.

I mean, no one is a bigger fan of my brother than me, but Krystina . . . when I laid eyes on her, I was so sure she was going to be a bimbo—and then she opened her mouth, and she's funny, and really clever. I think I might have a crush on her, too.

Please don't think I'm coming over all America-is-so-great when I've been in the country about ten minutes, but Americans seem to be a lot friendlier than British people. Krystina was sweet to me straightaway, and when I compare that to my first week in Sixth Form back in England, and how all the girls I didn't know looked at me suspiciously, and the only new boy who talked to me was the evil heartbreaker Luke, well, the Brits come off worse. Krystina was instantly offering to take me shopping with her, as if we were old friends.

"I've been *trying* not to buy these embroidered Earl jeans all month, and every day I get a *little* bit weaker," she said. "So you *have* to come with me to see them, and you *have* to say they're *horrible*, and then I won't buy them. Promise me you'll do that?"

"Er . . . yeah," I said. "But are they actually lovely?"

"Ohmigod. To. Die. For," Krystina said, rolling her eyes.

That's another thing about this place, though: everyone is rich—super rich. I've been hoping my dress sense looks like a British, boho sort of thing, rather than chain store, and I might just get away with it. A couple of girls admired my "cute shooooes!" and asked me where I got them before realizing that I was English, and it seems that Irregular Choice shoes, which cost fifty-five pounds back home (although I paid exactly half that in the sale) go for about a hundred and fifty dollars in tiny boutiques in New York, and are, like, totally far out. Ha-ha! I'm hip. Well, my feet are.

We went to a coffee shop and spread out in the corner, near the window, and Krystina talked a lot about an old British band, The Cure, and how she met the lead singer in New York one time. I hadn't heard of them, embarrassingly. I said I'd love to go to New York, especially as we were only an hour or so away, and Jeff started mumbling something about not being able to go this week. I couldn't help noticing how quiet Jeff was being. I thought he was in a bad mood at first, and then I realized he was quite tongue-tied around Krystina. I wanted to shake him and say, "Come on, Jeff, be funny!" but there was nothing I could do.

"So what are your plans, while you're here?" Krystina asked me. "You're coming shopping with me first, of course, and I think there may be a party this weekend for you to go to."

"Won't most people have gone home for the vacation, though?" I said.

"Well, there are still some people in town staying on to study and just hang out," Krystina said. "But it's a really nice atmosphere, because there's that end-of-semester feeling. And · it's hot and sunny. Not so much today, but believe me, it's gonna be."

Today it was already insanely hot. I'm not so good in extreme heat. I faint quite easily.

"And do you have a guy back home?" Krystina asked. "Anyone special?"

They say Americans are more direct. I didn't mind the question, but I was so anxious to seem like a light, funny person, and wanted to leave behind all my past with its broken hearts and failed romances.

"Not right now," I said, a bit stiffly. "I was thinking about having a fling while I'm here, though. Just a crazy, temporary holiday romance."

"Oh, yeah?" Krystina said. "Well, you're so pretty, that's not going to be difficult. I could call up five guys right now who'd love to interview for that opportunity. . . ." She looked at Jeff out of the side of her wide blue eyes. "But I think your brother might kill me if I did that. Let me know if anyone takes your fancy and I'll do my best to make it easier for you."

"Yeah, well," Jeff said, "*I'll* try and make it a bit more difficult. I'm the one getting a grilling from our mum every night about whether I'm looking after you, while you're still comatose from your jetlag at eight p.m. every night."

"I'm getting better!" I said. "I woke up at six this morning. That's nearly normal. Anyway, Jeff, you don't have to tell her *everything. . . .*"

"Yeah, you don't have to tell Mom *everything*, Jeff," Krystina said, playfully hitting Jeff on the arm. She looked pretty comfy with him. If he could just remember to *speak* every so often, maybe there is hope for him.

"Krystina's a bit gorgeous," I said casually to Jeff, when we were walking back home to his professor's house. The warm evening air was soft on my bare arms and legs, and I could have spent the whole night just walking outside. We'd stopped on the way to get ourselves a takeaway pizza.

"Does that mean you think I don't stand a chance?" Jeff asked glumly.

"Well, I think she definitely likes you," I said. "It may just be as a friend, I can't tell yet. Well . . . you know, maybe you should be a bit funnier around her—the way you are around me."

Jeff looked crushed. "What do you mean, 'funnier'?"

"Well, you know, usually you're really . . . lively, but today you were . . ."

"Boring?"

"No! Jeff, don't be nuts. You just seemed shyer than usual today."

"No, you're right," Jeff said, seeming to slump even lower. I felt horrible.

"There are good signs, too! I have more research to do."

"Don't say a word to her!" Jeff said, squeezing the pizza box anxiously. I was afraid he'd hurt the pizza. I put a steady hand on the box to keep it upright.

"I'm not going to say anything!" I said. "I'm quietly observing, that's all I'm doing."

"Don't even drop hints, Liv," he pleaded. "You're not as subtle as you think you are."

"The thing about you is, you think I'm still twelve years old and accidentally walking in on you snogging Sadie Fernandez when you were supposed to be babysitting me."

"And you told Mum!"

I gasped theatrically, pretending to be horrified that he hadn't forgiven me. "You can trust me now!" I squeaked. "We're both adults. I'm nearly eighteen, remember? I can vote soon."

"And that is truly frightening," Jeff said. "Er . . . remind me, who's the Home Secretary?"

"Ha! Well! As it happens, I have *already* made plans to find out who the Home Secretary is. *And* the Foreign Secretary."

"Oh, you're right," Jeff mocked, "the country is safe in your hands. It's good that you didn't waste all that time when you were stuck in hospital. And, how about naming the *Star Trek* movies, in order?"

"One: *The Motion Picture*, Two: *The Wrath of Khan*, Three: *The Search for Spock* . . . Just because I know this doesn't mean I don't know important polit–"

"Go on," he said, raising one eyebrow.

"Four: *The Voyage Home*, Five: *The Final Frontier*, Six. *The*

Undiscovered Country. Do you want me to do *The Next Generation* films, too?"

"Geek."

"Dork."

We were eating the pizza messily and greedily when the phone rang. Jeff wiped his hands, using *all* the paper napkins, and answered it.

"Hi, yeah. Oh, yeah, hi. Mm-hmm? Oh, yeah? Weeeeell . . . yeah, I don't think so. Yeah, I know my sister's still got really bad jetlag, so . . . Yeah, thanks, though, you and I've got to go for a coffee or see a film soon. Yeah. Ha-ha-ha-ha-ha! Yeah. Okay, see you."

He went straight back to stuffing more pizza in his mouth.

"Who was that?" I said.

"Huh? Oh, Adam. You remember the British guy you met at the cafet–"

"Yes, I remember, it was three days ago! What did he want?"

"He wanted to know if we wanted to go to a party round at his brother's tonight. I said you were too tired."

"But I'm not too tired!" I said.

"You've fallen asleep every night at eight!" Jeff said.

"I'm still setting my body clock to this time zone," I said.

"Well, you know," Jeff said, "his brother's older. I don't know what kind of party it's going to be. And you're going to take it easy for a bit."

"Je-*eff*, I've been taking it easy for years!"

"Okay," Jeff said, looking suddenly a bit more serious. He

put down the pizza slice—it was that serious. "I *am* going to take care of you while you're here, and I'm not taking you to every single party you get invited to, no matter what, until I know that you're up to it." We looked at each other, him trying to guilt me out, me not giving up. "Come on, Liv. I've been worried about you for a long time. Go easy on me."

"Yeah," I said, a bit sulkily.

"And it's only Adam," Jeff said. "You can see him in Manchester anytime you like."

"Yeah," I said, more bouncily. Although I was thinking, *Mustn't tell Jeff that I really quite like Adam. Like* like. "Okay, I'm going to check in with Mum now, and tell her that you're acting like an overprotective dad," I said, to try to lighten the atmosphere between us. I felt guilty for making Jeff feel bad.

"Oh, go on, please do that," Jeff said. "She'll love me for it. And while you're at it, tell her I *am* feeding you properly. . . ."

July 27

This morning gets an 8.5 on the weird-o-meter. I was having a frappuccino at the little coffee shop, reading *Heat!*, when I heard an English voice say, "Are you interested in English celebrities?"

It's a difficult question to answer "yes" to, even when "yes" is true. Who wants that to be the first thing they tell someone about their personality? I looked up at the face behind the voice: an incredibly thin boy, dressed in posh-boy clothes–lightly checked blue-and-white shirt with the sleeves rolled up, sand-colored trousers. He looked about twenty-one, had a floppy fringe of sandy-colored hair, and about ten more teeth than me. (Yes, I do have a full set of teeth. But he had more.)

I closed the magazine and looked at the cover, as if I'd forgotten what it was. "Oh, I brought it with me," I said. "I got here less than a week ago."

"You *are* English, then," the boy said, as if he was quite excited about it. He was really *insanely* skinny. His wrists were 2-D.

"Yep," I said. "I'm visiting my brother. He's getting some books from the library and then coming to meet me." I didn't mean it to warn him off, because it was quite nice talking to a stranger, particularly an English stranger.

"How long are you staying?" he said. "I'm Vaughan, by the way."

"Oh, Livia," I said, holding out my hand to shake hands and, as I always do when I do that, wondering if that was what I was supposed to do and whether he'd just stare at it and leave it hanging there. He shook it. "I've been here a week already, I'm here till August fifteenth, so a bit more than two weeks to go."

"How do you like it so far?"

"Hot!" I said, waving my hand in front of my face.

"Yeah . . . ," Vaughan said, and pulled at his collar with his little finger. Then there was a bit of chitchat, a bit of yes-I-like-that-too, and he explained that he was a PhD student, he was from London, and he'd just broken up with his girlfriend. I don't remember how he worked that last thing in. He asked if I'd been to the university art gallery yet, and I said I hadn't.

"How much time have you got?" Vaughan asked. "I'll show it to you right now, if you like."

"Is it near here?"

"Literally two minutes away."

I thought it might be nice and cool, art galleries always are. Well, you know, it wasn't that, it's just that I am useless at saying no, even to stick-thin Englishmen with too many teeth. So I said yes.

We were just reaching the gallery, and Adam came round the corner, nearly bumping into us. I must have done that thing where you reel in shock. I said, "Oh, hi!" very brightly, and then wondered if I should introduce the complete stranger I'd just met and agreed to go on a morning date with. Is there such a thing as a morning date? My "hi" had made Adam stop, so we'd all stopped, but no one had anything to say.

"I'm sorry we didn't go to your party," I said.

"Yeah, that's a shame," Adam said.

"I really wanted to go. My brother thought I was too tired."

"Oh—you didn't miss much," Adam said. "It was really Dougie's—my brother's—party. His friends." He looked straight at me after he'd finished speaking and I didn't have anything else to say either, I just wanted him to keep looking. He has this way of looking slowly at things, as if he's taking his own time to see them properly. It's quite intense, being looked at that way. Adam glanced at Vaughan and eventually said, "Well, see you later?" and walked off again, and I felt stupid and wished it was him I was walking into the art gallery with. I fancied him more today. It's those eyes, dark, like Luke's. Well, that's probably not a good sign.

Anyway, Vaughan and I were in the art gallery and I was waffling on about the amazing painting of a woman in red by Manet, trying to sound clever, and then I realized Vaughan's hand was on my bum. I'd thought, at first, that he was just standing too close, and maybe it was his leg somehow, but then I kind of checked out his position, and he moved it slightly and it was still definitely *on my bum*. And his head was really close to mine, as if he was smelling my hair.

So, what do you do when a boy you don't know very well

puts his hand on your bum? Well, if you're me, you're probably too polite to mention the fact that he's doing it. I said, "You know, now I think of it, I'd better get back in case my brother shows up, because I don't have my mobile, so he can't call me."

Vaughan took his long nose out of my hair.

"Okay," he said. "Shall I come back with you?"

"No, no need for that!" I practically shouted. "Better dash! Bye!"

As soon as I thought I was out of sight, I ran. I don't know why. Running isn't very cool in broad daylight, and outside the gallery it was intensely hot again. I just needed to run away. Sometimes you do. Anyway, I've been back here in this Internet shop since then, hiding out. Embarrassed. Time to update:

Things I know about love.

1. Nothing that happens between two people
is guaranteed to be private.

2. People don't always tell you the truth about how they feel.
And the truth is, it may not be the same as how you feel.

3. I don't know if you ever get over
having your heart broken.

4. Strangers are called strangers
because they are *strange*. Duh!

But thinking about the Vaughan episode, it sort of reminds me of a quote I always loved from *As You Like It*: "Come, woo me, woo me; for now I am in a holiday humour, and like enough to consent."

I *am* on holiday! You know, so what does it matter if I run into the odd crazy boy while I'm looking for a holiday romance? I'm here for fun. Bring it on. Only, from now on, maybe I should only consider Americans. I don't know why there are so many English boys in Princeton anyway! Well, three. But in my experience, the English boys I've dated have been (in order, and including today's art-gallery date) sad, bad, and mad.

Fancying Adam—which I do; he looked gorgeous today, all brown-skinned and twinkly-eyed and low-slung, crumply, jeansy—is allowed because he's my brother's friend, so not a serious option. I've always had crushes on my brother's friends. When I was about eight, I remember I was obsessed with one of them, called "Conk." Oh, Case Study . . . er . . . A-minus. I liked Conk because he was shorter than the others, sweet, and freckly. On Saturday afternoons I used to give him cookies I'd baked with my mum, which I always cut in the shape of flowers, with my little plastic flower-shaped cookie cutter. One day I found a cookie I'd given Conk earlier that day lying uneaten under a hedge. Jeff came in for a glass of orange soda, and I said he had to take out another cookie for Conk, and he said, "Why would he want another?" I said, "He must have dropped the one I gave him—it was under a hedge," and he said, "He always throws them away. He thinks they're horrible." Brothers are mean like that, when you're young. They punch you, and laugh at you, and tell you the truth. I could add another rule to my "Things I Know" list, something about the way boys lie, but even then, I realized that Conk just thought of me as a little sister who brought him yucky cookies and he hid them so as not to hurt my feelings. I've come to understand that my brother's friends are often cute, but are always somehow out of my league, even when they're not. They just don't think of me that way. It's nice that he's around, though.

Text from Krystina—she wants to go shopping tomorrow.

JULY 27

YEAH, this isn't good. I asked Livia and Jeff along to a party at my brother's and Jeff said they couldn't make it, Livia was jetlagged, blah blah blah, and today I saw her with this bloke, like a proper man-bloke, going into the art gallery. I don't know if she knows him from back home or if he's a friend of Jeff's, but the way he was looking at her, I think it's fairly clear that I've missed my chance. Which is a bit of a shame because the fact is, standing in the sun today, with that amazing hair shining—it was almost as if the sun was reflecting off her—she kind of took my breath away.

July 28

If you're ready for another recap of the "Things I Know" list, you'll have to wait, because I DON'T KNOW ANYTHING ABOUT LOVE. I wish I could read everyone's thoughts but keep my own private, but at the same time, have everyone know what I need them to know but without hurting their feelings and without risking my own feelings being hurt. Argh.

I ought to explain some of that.

"Okay, let me tell you where we're going first," Krystina said, when we pulled into a parking space in her white VW Rabbit (as they call it in the States) this morning. "The thing is, there's no point trying on beautiful clothes when you look and feel terrible, you just contaminate the clothes with your own . . . blah. And I look and feel blah. So you're coming with me to get a blow-out."

That's American for a blow-dry. But honestly, who pays to have someone dry their hair? Americans are constantly inventing new things to spend money on.

Krystina was looking incredibly sophisticated and cool—chilly cool—in a matching black cotton skirt and halter-neck top, both so unsweaty and unruffled that I was nervous following her into the hair salon wearing my raggedy denim mini and a simple pink T-shirt. But it is just so hot here that anything fancier—like my pretty silk top or my lovely, flowery sundress—would stick to me and crease. Denim doesn't show the sweat. Krystina and I were seated in adjacent chairs, and we had two quite noisy male hairdressers, called Guy and Paul. (*Me:* "Paul?" *Paul:* "Paah-oool." *Me:* "Er . . . Powell." *Paul:* "PAAAH-OOOL.") They discussed our looks together. Krystina said she just wanted a blow-out and I said, "Oh, me, too. Just a, um, blow . . . dry, please."

Paul shook his head. "Nah. I think we're gonna have to do a little more for you than a blow-out."

I said I didn't know about that because we had a lot of shops to get through.

"Oh, come on, a Paah-oool cut will take five minutes!" Paul said. "Straightening your friend's hair is going to take hours."

"He knows what he's talking about," Krystina said. "Don't you feel like a change, Livi?"

How did they know? Yes! More than anything! There's a kind of mad impulse that takes hold of me the second I sit in a hairdresser's chair. I just want to wave my hand at my head and say, "Make me look completely different!" And when it's all over, the moment they turn me around to face the mirror, I'll see this gorgeous, unrecognizable sexpot looking back at me. Instead, what usually happens is that the hairdresser insists on talking me through it and I gradually start to get more afraid. I nervously agree with them when they start talking about soft fringes and long layers, and then I walk out looking more or less the same as I did when I walked in, with the same straight fringe and long red hair. It suits me, I don't do anything to it, it's *me*.

"Your natural color is amazing," Paul said. "It's like your hair is telling you it wants to dazzle but you're not letting it." I blushed purple, because that's what I tend to do when people talk to me about me. Krystina was being led away to the shampoo area and I was left alone with Paul. He was making eye contact in the mirror and I was too afraid to pull away. "But I think sometimes you *want* to be noticed? The cut you have now is *sensible*. We're going to give you something closer to the way you feel. Keep some of the length, it's pretty. Probably keep these bangs, they suit you. But we'll chop into it a little? You think?"

I knew it was just going to look exactly the same. He's keeping the length, he's keeping the "bangs," spot the difference. My heart did sink a little bit, but I'd heard it before.

"Yeah, that sounds really nice," I said. You see, when I talk like that, with all the "that sounds really nice" and "just a blow-dry, please" stuff, it's not much of a surprise that I always end up with the safe option.

Paul talked about himself as he snipped away, and I relaxed, fascinated by the view in the mirror of Guy dragging the biggest straighteners I've ever seen along Krystina's hair—honestly, they were like oars. I felt quite ladylike, having my hair done with a friend, like characters in a 1950s film, and I started to get a sense of how different my life is right now, being here in Princeton, NJ, USA. Just a few weeks ago I was studying for my final exams with friends, passing round the popcorn while we asked one another test questions about parliamentary reform in the nineteenth century. Now my mum isn't around to worry about me, and there's only my brother keeping an eye on me. No one is going to talk me out of doing something by reminding me it isn't the sort of thing I do—the way my friends might. No one here is going to be surprised or freaked out if I don't seem myself because they don't know what that is. There's just a blank page for me to fill, every day.

"Shiny!"

Krystina's stylist, Guy, had walked over to take a look at the job Paul was doing on my hair, and he paused behind me with his arms folded. I looked up. My hair looked like red metal, and as Paul dried it in soft sections, I could see how fabulous the cut was. It was just resting on my shoulders rather than hanging a little below them, the fringe seemed to have grown longer (?) and was gently swept to one side, and the rest was this amazing dense mass of blunt layers that melted into one another when I shook them, making it look as if my hair was made up of lots of different shades. But it felt so light, and when I shook my head, it flew up and then fell back exactly into place, deliberately imperfect, a little bit edgy.

"What have you done?" I squeaked.

"Don't you think it's pretty?" Paul said.

"Oh my God, pretty? I *love* it!" I said. "I've never had good hair!"

"Are you kidding? People would kill for your hair."

"Oh, it's not the hair," I said, feeling really shy. "It's your cut. Thank you so much."

I had a quick reality check when Krystina came over to

admire it, too. She was glowing somewhere inside a halo of long, golden, film-star tresses.

"You look so beautiful," I told her.

"Yeah, yeah, we're cute," she said. "But we're not finished yet."

We went to a shopping mall next, and I thought how horrible it would be to go into artificial light on such a fantastic sunny day, but as soon as the air-conditioning hit me, I changed my mind. Cold, cold, fabulous cold, and suddenly my clothes felt looser and my face felt less shiny than my hair. Our first stop there was a department store, where Krystina sat us down at a makeup counter and let the orange-faced ladies give us a new look with "this season's summer palette." This was slightly less successful than the haircuts. We were trying not to giggle as we compared our amazing pearly finishes: they were sort of lovely and fairylike but, on the other hand, a lot too much like the makeup I used to wear to ballet recitals when I was six years old. We both left with a *sack* of free samples, burst out laughing when we were well away from the makeup department, and dared each other to keep it on all day.

Krystina was right, though. When you try clothes on and you feel a bit grubby and messy, everything looks wrong on you because you're too busy looking at your own flaws—but you don't *want* to look. When you're perfectly groomed and posh and pretty, you just can't stop looking at yourself, thinking, *I don't know if this can be true, but I look* great. I bought as many clothes as I could afford in preparation for coming to Princeton, and I have to make the money my mum gave me last the whole three weeks, but I bought one more dress this morning. It's black, with two-inch wide straps, but cut very high, almost like a slash-neck. It's really fitted on the bodice, then at the waist there's a fat gray bow and the skirt starts to stick out, just a bit wider than A-line. Very Audrey Hepburn. Not remotely old-me. But not so posh I couldn't wear it in the daytime with a little cardigan knotted at the waist. I love this dress so much that I never want to take it off. I almost made the woman pack up my scruffy old denim skirt in the bag so I could leave in it, but I knew I should save the dress for something special, just for its first time out in public.

At around six, we drove back into town and sat outside a café in the shade, sipping iced lattes, surrounded by all our bags. I was trying to look at my hair in my tiny little makeup mirror. In fact, I'd spent the whole day trying to catch sight of it in shop windows. This is my favorite haircut ever. I remembered I'd meant to ask Krystina more about how she felt about Jeff (but really subtly!), before I'd started getting totally seduced by the total body makeover she'd dragged me on. I tried to ease the subject into our conversation. Krystina was talking about how much she liked the songs Jeff had put on to her iPod, so I said, "Well, I think Jeff thinks you're amazing."

Okay, okay, that's not subtle at all. But Jeff should realize that there is no point leaving things unsaid forever when you only have a month left in someone's country. You have to let a girl know how you feel eventually or give up on her. Krystina tilted her head to one side and smiled.

"Really?"

"Well," I said, thinking I should give Jeff a chance to back out. "All I mean is, he's always talking about how cool you are— that's why I was so keen to meet you."

"Ahh," she said, and her smile stayed the same, but her eyes seemed to dim—or was I looking too hard? "Okay. Well, I think Jeff's amazing, too." Quite honestly, I just can't tell whether she likes him or not. Her phone rang, then.

"Yeah, yeah! We're here, come along now," Krystina said, hanging up. She turned to me and said, "Okay, there's someone coming and you're going to *love* me for bringing him."

At that exact moment, Adam walked in, and I was thinking, *Oh my God, does everyone know about this?*

Actually, it's really, really late and I've been typing for hours and can't concentrate, I need to write this properly tomorrow. I can hear Jeff snoring away in his bedroom and I'm yawning too much to see my screen.

July 29

I hope I still like my hair this morning. I'm looking at it now, but I just slept on it and bits are sticking up at the back. Hmm, but it brushes back into shape so easily. Yes, I still love it. Now, I need to finish off yesterday's entry.

Okay: there was cold coffee, me, Krystina, and Adam. I thought I'd mentioned him to her and hadn't *disguised* that I was interested in him, but things were moving too quickly! Adam came right over and a thought suddenly crossed my mind: if Krystina's here he's going to forget I'm in the room. But it was me he was looking at, smiling his little half-smile. He said, "Hey, how's your holiday going?"

"Hi. I love it here," I said—when I'm nervous I seem to be able to *hear* myself talking and my voice always sounds high, like a little kid's. "Do you two know each other, then?"

"Er, yes," Adam said. "We've met a couple of times . . . through your brother, actually. Krystina?"

Krystina smiled and nodded but didn't say anything to him, which seemed strange when she'd just called him and asked him to come along. And why didn't he seem to be sure of her name?

"How's everything going?" Adam asked me. "The hair is . . . Wow, your hair's great. Looks really good."

"Thanks," I said. "It's a lot easier to manage now. Less hot." *Come on, brain,* I was thinking, *be funny, be witty. Think of something good to say.*

"So, can I get you both another coffee or something?" Adam asked, hopping from one foot to the other and rubbing his palms together sideways—he looked a bit nervous and very cute.

"Oh, yes, please," I said. "Just a small peppermint tea, please."

"Green tea for me," Krystina said. "Thank you so *much.*"

When he'd gone, I said, "What? Why did you ask Adam to come? Does he know I fancy him?"

"I didn't ask *Adam* to come—I barely know the guy," Krystina said. "He just walked in. Princeton's a small town. You really *'fancy'* him?" She seemed amused by the word. Is it just a British word?

"Yeah, I'm starting to—I mean, I'm starting to *really* fancy him."

"Huh," she said absently, nodding. "But I thought you'd decided to have a fling with a foreigner." I glanced over at the line. Adam was looking down at his sneakers. I love his legs.

"I love his legs," I said out loud, without thinking, but Krystina didn't seem to hear me. It was probably such an incredibly crazy thing to say that she ignored it. "He was once really lovely to me, back in England, but I didn't know him, and I didn't think very much about it. But I feel that, you know, our paths crossing again all the way out here, that's weird, isn't it? And maybe it means something and maybe . . . Oh, gosh, wait, you said you'd invited someone along? Who was that?"

"My brother," Krystina said, and her face had brightened, but she was looking past me. "Kyle. He's just coming now. There he is."

A perfect, tanned blond jock walked past the coffee-shop window and pushed open the door. He quickly spotted Krystina and flashed us both two rows of the same ridiculously white and even teeth that his sister uses to break my brother's heart.

"Heyyyy," he said, striding across to us in two steps. "You must be Livvie. My sister's already told me you're a lot of fun."

You know what, I think you never want to be described as a lot of fun to anyone, particularly a boy. I think I'm *not* a lot of fun for one thing, and even if I were sometimes a *bit* of fun, "a lot" is too much to live up to.

"Well, I've been having a lot of fun with your sister," I said. "Oh, wow, you really look like each other."

"Hah-hah-hah-hah-hahhhhh," Kyle laughed, grabbing the spare chair and turning it backwards, then sliding himself into it, all in one graceful movement.

I looked up at Adam, who was still in line but was now talking to the server and not watching us. The place was full and I couldn't see any spare seats, and *as bloody usual*, as soon as I had the chance to speak to Adam, another bloke had popped up to sit in his place.

But Adam hadn't come in to see us, so maybe he didn't want to sit with us anyway. Still, as I watched the server laughing at whatever Adam was saying to her, I was growing more worried about the lack of space at our table when Adam came back. I'd stopped listening to Kyle and his weird giant's laugh, which seemed to come at the end of all his sentences. And at the end of all of my sentences. The laugh had a kind of "fee fi fo fum" quality.

"Do you want to have dinner with us tomorrow?" Kyle asked. "We're thinking of going to the Fish 'n' Chip shop. You can talk us through the menu." He said this in a ridiculously bad English accent that made me giggle. Kyle was encouraged by my giggling, adding, "Hah-hah-hahh!" I turned back to face him.

"I think Jeff is going to take me to the pictures tomorrow evening," I said, shrugging.

"The *pictures*? Do you live in the nineteen thirties? Hah-hah-hahhhh!" Kyle laughed.

"Er, I . . . ," I said.

"To the 'picture show'? Hah-hah-hahhhh!"

"Yeah, ha-ha, so I'm afraid I'm going to have to–"

"What are you seeing?" Krystina asked.

"The new Matt Damon film," I said, but my eyes had already traveled back to Adam, who was walking towards us now balancing the three drinks.

"I really want to see that, too!" Krystina said. "We can go in Kyle's car. Why don't we take you both?"

"Well, I could talk to Jeff about it. . . ."

Argh, this was too much pressure–I didn't like making decisions for other people, or turning people down. I really wasn't warming to Krystina's brother, Kyle. He seemed to be sort of an idiot; he was *very* loud, and he was making fun of me for being British all the time. By now Adam had come back with cups stacked on top of one another for me and Krys, only to find a big, yellow-haired boy sitting in between us.

"This is Krystina's brother," I said, as an explanation, not an introduction.

The boys both said "hey" to each other. Adam looked around for another chair, but I knew there wasn't one. Kyle started telling a long story about a friend of his getting drunk last week and just left Adam standing there, while I looked helplessly at him and didn't know where he'd go or what I should do. Could I have stood up next to him, leaned on a wall, and carried on where we'd left off before Kyle had turned up? Kyle was just going on and on, not seeming to notice the seating problem, or even that Adam was there.

I asked Adam if he wanted my seat. "I've been sitting for ages," I said.

Adam looked embarrassed. "No, no, I have to go actually, I just, you know, was on my way to the counter and saw you, so . . ."

"Oh," I said, nodding. "Well, if you have to go . . ." I didn't want him to go! He stood there for a minute, his eyes not leaving mine, and I couldn't think of anything else to say. I was feeling mortified that Adam had had to buy us drinks and then we hadn't *talked* to him, just thanked him and carried on listening to Krystina's brother telling his stupid story about drunk guys doing stupid things. I didn't know if Adam was going because he felt he was in the way, or whether he was upset or angry with me, or whether he only came over and bought us both drinks because I'd waved and smiled when he came into the coffee shop because I'd thought he was the person Krystina had invited.

The perfect girly day had turned into a disastrous boy day. And I was sad that I didn't like Krystina's brother as much as her, because I like her so much. Shopping with her yesterday was fantastic fun. I must try harder to like Kyle.

I might talk to Jeff about some of this when he wakes up, although I shouldn't tell him how I'm beginning to feel about Adam—they're friends, it'd freak him out. It's a breathtakingly beautiful morning—at this time of day, before it starts to get really hot, the sun is clear and the daylight is a sort of shell-pink color. Everything seems shiny and clean and unspoiled, and it's easy to hope the things I did yesterday that were messy will just be swept away today.

blogplace: Inside Adam

JULY 29

IT'S NOT exactly unexpected that someone as attractive as Livia is going to be surrounded by blokes, but she is *always surrounded by blokes.* I walked into the coffee shop yesterday and she was there. I thought I'd get a chance to have a bit of a chat with her and her friend, maybe try to be a bit funnier than I was the last time I saw her, stretch out the old Adam charm, you know. It is there; it's just resting. So I went to get her a drink, and by the time I'd got back—we're talking three minutes?—some Brad Pitt is sitting on a chair the wrong way round and laughing at her jokes. The weedy English bloke at the gallery was one thing, but I'm starting to think she's well out of my league. The fact is, I don't know if she's into either of them, so I'm not going to give up. Anyway, I've already e-mailed Jeff to ask if they fancy coming out this evening. Jeff said they're going to see a movie at six but he and Livia can be back in town for about nine. So that's good, right?

July 29: Part 2

I was getting ready for Krystina and Kyle to turn up to take us to the pictures–trying to straighten my hair to get it as shiny as Krystina's–and Jeff came in eating a carrot like Bugs Bunny and said, "Oh, hey, I told Adam–d'you remember Adam, that bloke you–?"

"Yes, of course I remember Adam! What?"

He chomped on the carrot for a few annoying seconds. "Oh, yeah, I told Adam we'd maybe meet up with him for dinner after the film, if that's okay with you. If you're tired, it's no problem. It's just I've had to turn down seeing him a bit recently and I'd like to catch up. But it's totally up to you."

"No, that's fine," I said coolly. "Yeah, it'd be nice to see more of him, sure."

"I'm going to get another carrot. You fancy one?"

"No, thanks."

"We won't be eating for hours."

"I'm fine, thank you."

"Mum keeps asking me if you're getting all your fresh veggies, you know."

"All right, give me a bloody carrot!"

I spoke to Mum this afternoon, just before she went off to work. It's more than a week since I saw her, and I've never spent so much time away from her. She was on the webcam and I'd never seen her on it before and not been in the same room. She was there in the corner of my screen, smiling at me, thousands of miles away. I know that I'm coming up to the point in my life where I will properly leave home—but thinking about that still makes me very nervous and sad . . . and panicked, as if I suddenly might forget how to make my heart keep beating. Anyway, she was putting on a lovely, sunny voice, and telling me funny stories about the people at work, but I could hear a kind of strain in her voice, as if she wanted to cry. I love it out here, but I wish I could just go back every couple of days (sometimes, I wish I could go back every night) and hug my mum.

Kyle is a weird driver in that he goes slowly but you never feel safe. He shouts a lot at other drivers, and surely you don't usually find that many people driving that badly on a fifteen-minute drive? He also constantly turned to look at me when he was talking to me—I was sitting in the passenger seat, Jeff and Krystina in the back—and I wished he'd keep his eyes on the road. Behind us, my brother and my new friend seemed to be getting on a lot better. They were talking in low voices, Krystina giggling at whatever Jeff was saying. I realized that to give Jeff some time to impress her, I'd have to do my best to get on with Kyle, and "take one for the team"–Jeff started using that expression when he first came out here. He and I *are* a team. I'm so happy about this: his friendship is one of the best things in my life.

I was relieved, though, when we pulled into the cinema car park and joined up as a four again. Jeff bought the tickets to thank Kyle for the lift. Kyle bought a gigantic bucket of popcorn for us all to share. I ended up sitting between him and Krystina– Jeff was on Krystina's other side–and we passed the popcorn up and down our little line the whole time, which became a bit distracting when I was trying to follow the film. But there was something more distracting than popcorn to contend with. Kyle had laughed a lot in the coffee shop, but that turned out to have been only been a small hint of what he was capable of. Here in the cinema, Kyle laughed his giant's laugh at every single joke and–just for fun–at lots of lines that weren't jokes at all. On my right, Krystina was leaning the other way, her head resting on Jeff's shoulder. I sat up very straight.

"So, you seemed to like the film," I said to Kyle, as we were walking out together.

"Not that much, not really," Kyle said. "It was full of clichés, old jokes, kind of predictable. It was okay, nothing special."

Right, exactly how insane is he? Who laughs like that at a film they don't like?

I was hoping we'd be able to lose them when we went to meet Adam at the Indian restaurant as we'd arranged, but I knew Jeff wouldn't want to say good-bye to Krystina so early, so we all piled in together. Adam was already sitting down at a big table, and I felt embarrassed about coming in with Kyle. I wanted him to know we hadn't come *together*, but as far as I knew Adam didn't care one way or another.

"How was the film?" Adam asked me, shuffling along the bench to make more room for me. I sat down right next to him. I just had a clear, selfish moment, where I thought: *No one can stop me and I want to sit here.* And I was suddenly close to him for the first time since working out how I felt about him, and my heart started beating heavily. So how *was* the film? I'd spent most of it thinking about Kyle's embarrassing bellowing laughter.

"It was quite a . . . *noisy* experience," I said, glancing at Kyle and emphasizing it a bit crazily, hoping Adam would pick up that I wasn't talking about the film.

"Are you talking about the film . . . or the *audience*?" Adam said, with the same emphasis and also glancing at Kyle—so he had!

"The audience," I said, and checked to see that Kyle wasn't listening to us. He was on my other side—the three of us were sitting opposite Jeff and Krystina—but Kyle was caught up with telling the other two about the last time he'd come to this restaurant with some friends, and one of them got drunk and behaved badly. He didn't seem to have noticed I wasn't listening, because he turned round to smile at me while he was laughing at one of his own jokes.

"Talking through important scenes?" Adam said.

"No, not talking," I said. "Although, it was quite disturbing."

"Was it . . . laughing, maybe? Could it have been quite

loud laughter?" Adam said, and at that exact moment, Kyle exploded with his usual giant's mirth. I waited for him to stop.

"Yes, that was the exact problem," I said. "So, as you can imagine . . ."

". . . it was quite hard for you to concentrate," Adam finished. And then he smirked and I smirked, and his dark eyes were full of mischief, and even though I'd known for days that I'd been tumbling head over heels for him, this was the very first moment that I knew he and I were thinking the same thing, and he liked me, too.

We didn't flirt or anything after that—Adam was talking to Jeff a lot, Kyle was telling long stories that he didn't like to be interrupted in the middle of, Krystina was telling me how great my hair looked. But when we all walked out to go our separate ways, Adam put his hand on my arm and gently pulled me back.

"Are you free tomorrow?" he said.

"Yes."

"All tomorrow?"

"Yes," I said. "I have no plans all day."

"Meet me for breakfast," he said, but not like it was a question, and I just wanted to *laugh* with happiness.

"Yes, where?"

"The Student Center, nine o'clock." And then he smiled. "You're really going to come?"

"Yes," I said, and then I skipped ahead to get level with my brother and Krystina, and he turned and went in the other direction.

Things I know about love.

1. Nothing that happens between two people
is guaranteed to be private.

2. People don't always tell you the truth about how they feel.
And the truth is, it may not be the same as how you feel.

3. Strangers are called strangers
because they are *strange*. Duh!

4. I think you can get over a broken heart. If you start getting
obsessed with someone else, you forget that it hurts.

JULY 30

I'M NOT sure how that happened. She walked in with the Laughing Brad Pitt, and I thought, *Oh, that's the way it is, okay, fair enough.* But then she sat down next to me, and when she was talking about going to the pictures with him, she kind of made fun of him, and I wasn't sure I'd read it right so I took it slowly. But there's kind of a rule: you don't start chatting up a girl in front of her brother. Having said that, Jeff doesn't seem to know about that rule—and Brad Pitt's sister seemed pretty interested in him yesterday. It'll never last, though. He's just some English bloke and she's an American Blonde. Still, Gwyneth Paltrow, and all that.

I'm seeing Livia in half an hour. Just me and her, no brothers, no Mr. Brad Pitt, no freakishly skinny English blokes. Just her and her amazing smile, the one that makes me crumple up inside. I've got a few plans for today, a couple of ideas about how I should play this, if I don't lose my nerve. But I'll see how it goes.

July 31

Adam was leaning against the wall of the cafeteria when I turned up ten minutes early. He stopped leaning when he saw me and came over. I was wearing my new black Audrey Hepburn dress, with a little pale yellow cotton cardigan on top, and my hair in a messy bun that had taken me about half an hour to get right.

"Wow, you're seriously punctual," he said. Punctual? Ahem! What about my dress?

"So are you."

"How about . . . ?" He smiled, a bit naughtily. "How would you feel about taking a *slightly* later breakfast in New York?"

It was one of those moments where I was having too many emotions at once, so I couldn't think straight. The main one was silly, giddy, delirious delight. Jeff had been so busy working, he *still* hadn't made a plan with me to go there, but I could almost *feel* New York from Princeton, it was so close—living, breathing, tempting me, drawing me there. The most glamorous city in the world—that's got to be a good first date. And to go there for *breakfast*! Like we were just, you know, the sort of people who went to New York for breakfast. "Yes!" I shouted.

There were other emotions and thoughts elbowing one another for space in my head. The ones that said, *No. It's scary. I need to tell my mum. I need to tell Jeff. How well do I know him? What if something happens? What if we get lost? What if we get killed? Don't do it!* I knew that my mum would be furious if I went without telling Jeff, *and* she probably wouldn't let me go without him.

"Great. Give Jeff a ring and let him know—ask him if he thinks you should go, actually," Adam said, interrupting my thoughts as if he could actually hear them and was getting fed up with listening to them natter on. "We can wander down to the train station and you can call while we're waiting, and if he thinks it's a bad idea, you'll have got to see the university train station. And that's really a tourist attraction in itself."

At the tiny station—barely more than a little platform and a stationmaster's hut—I sat down on a bench and called Jeff. Adam gave me space, walking down to the other end of the platform and leaning against a metal lamppost there. I looked at him in his light blue T-shirt with navy blue stripes down the arms, a pair of bluish canvas jeans hanging loose on his gorgeous thin legs, his dark hair shiny in the morning sun.

"Hi, Liv," Jeff said. "Everything okay?"

"Adam thinks we could go to New York today. What do you think?"

There was a short silence. Not good. "Do you want to go?"

"Oh, Jeff, yeah—so much."

"How do you feel?"

"What do you mean?"

"You know what I mean, Livvie."

"Jeff, I'm not sick anymore," I said, lowering my voice.

"That doesn't mean you're strong enough to act like you're exactly the same as everyone else. You get tired." Jeff sighed. "But yeah, it's just a little train ride, and then a walk around town. He's not exactly going to take you rappelling down the Empire State Building." (At the mention of the Empire State Building, my heart went fluttery.) "It's going to be a nice day for it, too—cooler. The weather says there's even a chance of a little light rain."

"So, are you saying you approve?" I said.

"No, I don't really *approve*," Jeff said. "But you're going anyway, aren't you? Livia, promise me you'll take it easy. Don't run around. Don't sit in the sun. Don't do too much. Adam's a good bloke—*tell* him as soon as you're feeling tired, and tell him why. You don't have to go on about it, just let him know. And don't come home too late. And I'll take you properly next week, if you don't mind going with me."

"Of course I want to go with you!" I said. "More than anyone! Jeff, you're great. Are you going to tell Mum?"

"Yes," Jeff said.

"What? She'll only worry. Why?"

"Because we're grown-ups, Liv, we don't try to hide stuff from Mum anymore."

The train was like something out of another era—the stationmaster waited till everyone who wanted to come on board was on, and then seemed to set off when he fancied it. Adam said this train was called "the Dinky" by locals.

"The local kids used to 'surf' on the top of it," Adam said.

"What, you mean, actually standing on the top of the train?" I said. "What if they fell off and got killed?"

"One did."

"Blimey!" I said, and tried to look up and around the window to check there were no kids jumping on. There were sweet, little squashy leather seats, and only a few passengers. Sadly, we wouldn't be taking the Dinky all the way—we had to change five minutes later at Princeton Junction. The second train was much bigger and less cute, packed with more serious people. Everyone looked so foreign—American. Even the little old ladies didn't look anything like British little old ladies—they had bigger hair, smarter clothes, and more jewelry. Adam tucked our tickets in the edge of the seat and passed me a bottle of cold water, and I leaned back and looked out the window.

We were chatting about silly stuff; I was helping him catch up with what had been going on in the British celebrity world since he'd been away, and the gentle normality of it all was relaxing me. I was reminding myself this was just like going to Manchester from Liverpool: just a city at the end of a train ride, and another train ride home. What had I been panicking about? Just a fear of the unknown. So, despite Jeff's warnings, I didn't think I needed to give Adam the whole history of my-life-as-an-ill-person on my first real date with him.

"Those don't look too much like walking shoes," Adam said, looking down at my little black sandals. "We'll be taking it easy, I think."

"They're fine," I said. "They're almost flat. I can walk miles in these."

"I can't believe you just agreed to come with me to New York," Adam said, shuffling lower in his seat and smiling.

"Why?" I said. I turned all the way to the side to look at him.

"Well, breakfast is one thing, but you're going to have to spend hours with me now," he said, his eyes twinkling.

"Yeah, I didn't think of that—what if we run out of things to say?" I said, pretending to be worried. I don't know why this seemed so funny, because in the real world, I am *constantly* worrying about running out of things to say to people—but it did seem funny, all the same. Adam is just ridiculously easy to talk to. "And I don't know my way around the city, so I'll have to hang out with you all day."

"That could be a problem . . . ," Adam said, rubbing his chin. "What about if we just turn back as soon as we get there? You said you liked riding on trains, so this is *already* probably the best date of your entire life."

I wanted to giggle, but I kept my voice serious. "Well, I suppose we could just take a look around for *five* minutes," I said. "Just to get the value out of our train tickets. But then yes, let's come straight back. Before the conversation completely dries up."

Adam laughed, and then—oh, wow—then he kissed me. Just a tiny, quick kiss on the lips.

"Sorry, I couldn't resist," he said. "You're really funny. You're absolutely beautiful."

Instantly, I could feel my eyes fill with tears and my skin start to go pink. I turned my face away from him quickly while I tried to hold in my emotions. I hadn't felt quite like this before. No one had ever said anything as sweet to me. Luke had always been quite mean; right from the beginning, he'd always said very funny, but slightly cruel, things—what exactly *had* I found so irresistible about that? And when I turned back to Adam, he kissed me again, and it was just as surprising—but this kiss was a few seconds longer, gentler, and we ducked lower than the seatbacks so no one could see. I hadn't been kissed in a long time. It's sort of shocking, the closeness of someone's face, as though they're suddenly more real.

"Well," Adam said, leaning back and sighing, "I've got that out of my system now. I can leave you alone for the rest of the day. I always say, if you kiss the girl at the start of the date, it takes the pressure off."

"Oh, really, is that what you *always* say?" I said.

"Always. It's my golden rule. I've literally been saying it since . . . since I met you again in Princeton. Well, I suppose it came a bit after that. I've definitely been saying it all morning."

We were still making jokes as we talked, but my eyes were more serious, searching his for reassurance—this really was as good as it felt, wasn't it? Were we moving too quickly?

Luke who?

Let me tell you what it felt like to see New York for the first time: it's a film. I've walked into a film. There really is steam coming up from the circles in the pavement, and men are really leaning out of delivery vans shouting, "Hey, lady! Get outta the way!" and women in posh suits are walking into the street whistling for cabs and eating pretzels in paper. And it's *too tall*. I just had to stand still and stare with my mouth open and I wanted to laugh out loud.

"Are you ready to eat?" Adam asked.

"Well, I always say, if you eat at the start of a date . . ."

"Okay, okay. Let's eat."

We walked downtown from the train station to Chelsea, and it was already too hot for my cardigan. I felt just a little nervous exposing my shoulders, but caught my reflection in a window, and was amazed to see I looked quite ladylike. The place where we had breakfast was a bit like an English tearoom—lots of dark-wood-framed windows, and wooden tables very close together. I had French toast—thinking it would be toast-sized—but it came looking like two hardback books gently fried in butter and dusted with powdered sugar. I still managed to eat most of it.

"I don't know if you have places you want to see first," Adam said. "I'll take you anywhere you want to go. But also, if you'd rather just take it easy and trust me to have a plan, well, I have a sort of plan."

"I think we should go with your plan," I said.

"Well, it's not a *plan* plan," he said, laughing. "I think I should get you to sign a disclaimer, agreeing that if you go with my plan you can't turn around later and say, 'Call that a plan?'"

"I'm not signing anything!"

"But I've already prepared the papers! Look, would you like me to go through my plan, and you can raise your objections now?"

I fixed him with a straight look. "Adam, you could take me on a tour of the city sewers and I would just be so happy to be here. Please don't worry about your plan."

"Yeah, the plan is approved!" he said, making a celebratory fist.

The plan involved walking under shady trees on the Lower East Side and talking, and laughing, and accidentally walking into each other when we were trying to look up at the prettiest buildings. Kids were playing basketball on courts boxed off with wire fencing, and we hopped off the pavement to let a tall old man with slightly blue hair get past us with his three shaved poodles. A scratchily written sign saying, YARD SALE led the way to a kind of informal street market, where Adam insisted on buying me a 1960s board game, which made me squeak with delight when I saw it, called Cocktail Time. It had little plastic martini glasses as pieces, and color picture cards of sophisticated ladies in sticking-out dresses and party food to collect—it cost him a mighty four dollars. Now, I don't know about you, but I didn't know that going out with boys could be quite this easy. Aren't you supposed to have more agonizing "Does he like me?" time before you're walking around New York with him? Shouldn't you hide your feelings for longer, in case he's freaked out and scared off by your keenness?

"I don't know if you like clothes shops and things," Adam said, "but this little street has the kind of shops I thought seemed sort of your style—although I could have got that really wrong, so don't be offended."

When I came to New York with Adam, I thought it'd all be about giant department stores—Macy's and Bloomingdale's, with glass elevators and liveried doormen. But Adam was taking me through the small, personal streets, the places he'd discovered and kept for himself. These little shops weren't very expensive, but they were filled with jewelry made from delicate crystals, and old photographs, vintage prom dresses in rainbow pastels, new clothes by hip student designers, and in one, a pair of shiny red shoes that almost looked like Dorothy's from *The Wizard of Oz*. In a cruel twist of fate, they were in my size. But I couldn't afford them, and they were far too impractical.

"They're not really any less sensible than the ones you've got on. How are your feet holding up in those strappy things, by the way?" Adam asked me.

"I told you, I can walk for miles in these."

"You have walked for miles in them now. Come on, let's stop for a drink."

It was about five o'clock, and we ate cupcakes with homemade lemonade in a little bakery with only a few tables and a snowy white cat who sat in the corner, licking its paws and watching us with its green eyes. My feet *were* tired, and I was tired, too. I remembered what Jeff had said. My feelings for Adam had grown deeper over the day. I could talk to him about myself, I could tell him a half-truth—and not keep hiding everything from him. I've started to trust him, but when I think about what happened with Luke, maybe that's a mistake. It's so *unfair*—that the cancer still has the power to ruin my life even when I've nearly got all the way through it. I was picking crumbs of icing off the sides of my cupcake wrapper, and wondering how you can ever tell someone you're different—damaged—without them being completely freaked out and running a mile.

"What's wrong?" Adam asked. "You look sad. Is that cat bothering you? Because I'm not afraid of it. I'll go and tell it to stop staring." The cat flicked its tail with annoyance, as if it had heard him.

"No, it's not."

"If you want me to," he added, frowning as if he was trying to read my mind. I looked into his brown eyes and couldn't speak. "I think I'd do more or less anything you wanted me to do today," he said quietly, then more loudly, "Well, before you get any ideas, not murder. It'd probably take quite a lot of persuading for me to get involved in a murder for you. Even some kind of robbery, I'm not really sure about that. Let's just rule out crime of any kind right now, in fact."

I was too tired to laugh. I gave him a weak smile.

"You want to go home, don't you?" Adam said.

"No," I said. "Of course not. I'm just tired."

"Well, anyway, let's get you home," he said. "We'll come back again soon. This is turning into quite a long breakfast date. You could sue me under the Trade Descriptions Act."

"It's lucky I refused to sign anything, then," I said. And I chickened out of telling him. We had just missed the train when we got to the station, and as we waited for the next one, we seemed really to have finally run out of things to say, and my head felt too woolly and tired to do any better. Finally we boarded, and I took out my lovely Cocktail Time set and we talked about that for a while until, lulled by the steady rattle and gentle rocking motion of the train, I silently leaned against him, and he put his arm around me and, nearer to Princeton, when the carriage emptied, we kissed and kissed. We didn't get back until after nine. He walked me home in the opposite direction to the evening's lilac sunset, and I said he ought to come in and say hi to Jeff.

I opened the door with the spare keys Jeff had given me, and when we got inside, we were more than a bit surprised to see Jeff and Krystina snogging on the sofa.

blogplace: Inside Adam

JULY 31

THANK GOD for the train ride home. At that point, I was seriously worried. For most of the day, I'd been doing very well. I mean, really, you should have seen me. I made a couple of okay jokes, she seemed to like the flea market, I took her to look at shoes . . . but at some point in the day I might have actually bored her to death. But then she was opening up her game on the train, and getting excited about it in that ridiculously cute way of hers, and it happened.

I am besotted with Livia Stowe.

August 1

"*My brother* was really into you, you know," Krystina said, mock-scoldingly. "I didn't know you were already interested in someone else." I say *mock*, but I wasn't sure there wasn't a bit of spikiness hiding under her smooth, teasing voice.

"That's not true," I protested. "About him being into me, I mean. He didn't really have any time to get to know me."

"Well, you're very cute. You could have told me you were serious about Adam earlier. You knew, didn't you?"

"Sort of, yes, but I didn't know I stood a chance with him."

I looked up at her to see if she was really angry about all of this. Krystina rolled her eyes.

"Oh, come on. Anyway, I forgive you, and besides, both of us dating the other's sibling would have been *too weird*. And I'm very crazy about your gorgeous, annoying brother."

"Now *that* I still can't believe," I said. "He's been mad about you since he met you."

"I just didn't know I stood a chance with him," she said, and gave me a pointed look. Well, sure, it sounded crazy when *she* said it. But you should see her.

We were sunbathing on one of the grassy squares between the college buildings. I say *we*—Krys was lying there in a crocheted red bikini top and short blue shorts looking like Wonder Woman, baking herself a deeper shade of honey, sitting up now and again to tell me off, while I was smothered in SPF50, with a sun hat, sunglasses, and a lot of cotton clothing. Ginger hair, you know the score.

I've been missing my friends from back home.

Not because I'm unhappy—the opposite. I want them to associate me with good news, too. You know how I'd been worrying about having lost out on some of the closeness they shared, because of my illness? Before I came to Princeton, I'd been feeling more and more as if I was living in a different time from them, as if I'd been held back a few years—which in many ways I had. When they talked about nightclubs, I'd think, "You go to *nightclubs*? What are you, *women*?" and then remember that we all sort of are. They'd been there for me when I broke up with Luke, but that had been the last time since my illness that I'd had anything different to talk about, and it was all a long time ago. They'd given me lots of support and reassurance and I'd felt loved and supported, but the news, as it always was with me, had all been bad.

I do constantly worry about how to tell Adam the things he doesn't know, and what to tell Adam, and what I'll do if it makes him see me another way. It's too soon for me to be scared about this . . . and yet, I know that what I feel for Adam is the most exhilarating and amazing thing I've ever felt. I remember being happy in the early days with Luke, but this is different. I don't feel insecure this time. I don't have reservations about *him*, the way I did with Luke—Luke was always addictively attractive, but he was also nasty about my friends, and the way he joked with me often went beyond the point where it still seemed like a joke. I found myself making a lot of excuses for him and keeping a lot of things a secret. It's as if I'm only just noticing this now, but I always thought it and didn't dare think *about* it. Right from the start there were moments when I just didn't even *like* him.

I know lots of girls say "but this is different" before they get their hearts broken, again. But this is *nothing* like my last relationship. There is nothing I don't love about Adam. Just in little ways: the way he talks about his brother and how much he cares about him—and understands how I feel about mine. The way he looked at my sandals and worried that my feet might start to hurt. The way he took me to the shops he thought I'd love—and got it right. Luke used to drag me round endless record shops to show me bands I'd never heard of because he said I had terrible taste and I needed to be told what was good.

In big ways, there's no comparison. Adam's type of funny isn't mean or biting. His dark brown eyes are kind. He's quicker to get what I'm talking about, maybe because he's cleverer, maybe because we're more like each other, or maybe just because he's more interested and *wants* to understand. He thinks I'm funny. And this might sound hopelessly girly and lame and gullible (those are Luke words, that's what he'd say) but it was *really* nice when Adam told me I was beautiful. Because I'm so obviously not! I'm a mess. I have stupid hair and I'm pale and freckly and my nose is too fat and my eyelashes are white and my thighs are too big and my knees hit each other when I walk and oh God let's not go into all the other stuff . . . and *he thinks I'm beautiful.*

Comparing them is all wrong, because it makes it sound as if I'm not properly over Luke, as if he's still on my mind. When I think of Luke now, though, I don't feel anything–not bitter, not empty, just like clouds floating on a soft summer's day, lying in a field feeling light-headed and careless. The thought of him making me as sad as he did seems *insane.* If I think of him at all, it's just to think, what the hell was I *doing* with him? I'm proud of Adam. He can meet my friends and I can relax. I won't worry about him being sullen and sneering and saying the wrong thing and I don't have to dread hearing what he's saved up to tell me later. And yeah, this feeling is why I'm craving my friends' company. Because I'm happy, and I want them to know me happy!

The mad sequence of events from the previous couple of days had jolted my friendship with Krystina and, as we were sun-bathing together, I could sense there'd been a change between us. She's now my brother's girlfriend–which means I'll see more of her, but I won't be the person she's coming to see anymore. We have to like each other for his sake, as well as our own. This is going to sound nuts, but whereas our friendship was natural and easy from the moment we met, now I'm saying things and thinking, *I hope I don't make Jeff sound bad,* and *I hope she doesn't think our family is awful.* There had been a kind of subtle pressure for me to get on with her brother, and that pressure has been completely removed now that I've been spending time with Adam. But all the same, I'm worrying more and more about Kyle turning up, just because I think it would be embarrassing. And now that I see *even more* of Krystina, because of Jeff, there's *even more* chance of running into Kyle again. Ack, what a mess!

"By the way, there's a party on Saturday," Krystina said. "I thought we could all go?"

"Oh, er . . . what did you have in mind?" I said. Could I still bring Adam or was she too cross about the fact that I'd secretly started seeing him without telling her?

"It's like a big communal party—a lot of the guys in Butler are planning to open up their apartments and set it all up in the spaces between them, play some music, have some fun. . . ."

The Butler Apartments are a little village of "temporary" student houses, except Krystina says they've been there about fifty years. Jeff had told me they were full of graduate students, i.e., older than all of us, and a lot older than me. I was quite apprehensive.

"But would they mind if we turned up uninvited—me and, er . . . Jeff and . . ."

"No, of course not! Well, ask Adam if he wants to go when you next see him."

I met Adam later for lunch at a sushi bar. Out of nowhere, when I saw him standing outside, waiting for me, I felt a stab of fear that made me want to run away. Yesterday in New York had been so perfect, but what if it had meant more to me than him? It was possible that everything I'd thought about since yesterday, all the daydreams of him meeting my friends, that it was all me getting carried away, summer madness. Holiday romance. Maybe it hadn't been the same for him. Maybe he hadn't even pretended it had, and I'd only heard what I wanted to hear. In this moment, when I was a few seconds away from finding out how he'd start talking to me today, and whether everything would be fine, I suddenly felt cold and alone. I wanted a backup plan and more time to make sure of what I'd been feeling all morning. I wanted the confidence back. Adam just smiled his little half-smile and didn't say anything at first. He came up to me and held out his hand, and when I took it, he kissed me . . . just a tiny kiss, but somehow it said what I needed to hear. And everything was okay.

"You look really pretty," he said, and touched my back lightly as he let me go into the sushi bar in front of him.

The Japanese owner of the bar was comically bossy and made fun of our English accents.

"You're English, yes? I bet you like your sushi cooked well done," he said, and laughed loudly. "Maybe you'd like it boiled?" His chef, who was slicing the salmon, rolled his eyes and grinned at us.

"Krystina's asked us if we fancy going to a party tomorrow at the Butler Apartments," I said to Adam, snapping my chopsticks in two. "What do you think?"

"Well, yeah, those parties are supposed to be great fun," Adam said, nodding. "But I won't know many people there. Would Jeff be going?"

"Yeah."

"We could have a good time, then," Adam said. "And I'm

free and I'd like to see you, so yes." I realized that I was almost disappointed, because it would mean an evening out with him that wasn't really all about us, that we couldn't make up as we went along. Adam looked at me. "What's up? Don't you want to go?"

"I'm not so great at parties when I don't know many people there."

"You don't have to be great at parties. You'll know me and Jeff. And Krystina. I'm sure Kyle'll pop up, and he's a laugh a minute."

I hit his arm with the back of my hand. "Oi."

"We don't have to go," Adam said. "I said yes because I thought it was what you wanted. But I don't mind either way. If you'd prefer, you and I can sit outside on Dougie's balcony and watch for shooting stars." As soon as he'd said it, I knew that was what I wanted to do. "Let's go," Adam said, apparently not reading my mind at all. "You need to know that parties aren't scary. It'll be fun."

August 3

It's two weeks today since I came to America, and less than two weeks till I go, again. Adam just walked me home, and Jeff is asleep. I don't know what happened to him after we left the party. I texted him to let him know I was going to stay over at Adam's brother's apartment, and he just texted back, OK. That is an awkward text to have to send to your brother. You have to keep it short. You can't send something like: THAT DOESN'T MEAN ADAM AND I ARE GOING TO DO ANYTHING, YOU KNOW, WELL EVEN I DON'T KNOW BUT WELL OBVIOUSLY WE'RE GOING TO DO SOMETHING BUT NOT WHAT YOU THINK BECAUSE I'M DEFINITELY NOT READY FOR THAT YET BUT DON'T THINK ABOUT IT TOO MUCH EVEN THOUGH I AM.

Yesterday was another soft, balmy night, and Krystina, Jeff, Adam, and I walked to the Butler party together. A few of the little aluminum apartments were completely open, and people were going in and out. There was dance music blaring out of a big sound system. In one apartment, the bathtub was full of ice, and there were drinks sticking out of it—mostly beers, some sodas. We ran into Kyle by the Coke machine; he was rocking it from side to side and laughing, and it wasn't clear whether he was trying to claim a legal bottle of Sprite or thought he'd worked out a way of stealing from it. I was actually pleased to see someone I knew because there were a lot of older people I *didn't* know wandering around and I'd felt out of place since I got there and knew I didn't want to stay. We would have gone earlier, but it became clear pretty soon on that Jeff might be bit stranded if we did.

The first thing that happened was that Krystina started dancing, and Jeff has never been much of a dancer, so he stayed with me and Adam—we stood in a line talking about the music and watching her. At the beginning she pulled me over with her by my wrists, but no one else was really dancing, although a couple of girls in groups were standing around sort of moving to the music. I felt very stupid—I was one of the youngest people here, and dancing seemed to draw attention to that. I retreated to Adam and Jeff, and Krystina came to pull me back again, but I smiled and shook my head, knotting my arm with Adam's. She went back to dancing, losing herself in the music, her hands winding imaginary ribbons above her head, her eyes half-closed. We stayed with Jeff, but there was something about this that seemed wrong and made me feel bad for him. A boy I'd never seen before, indie-kid looks—dyed black hair, a silver spike piercing just under his lower lip, and a few heavy silver chains around his wrist—but very attractive, started dancing with her.

I could hear Krystina shouting to him over the music, "Trey!

Have you got some of *your* music? Can they put on some of *your* music, Trey?"

The boy felt in his pockets and shook his head.

"Oh, yeah, that's got to be Trey," Jeff said, nodding. "He's the singer in a band she likes—the Psycho Rats."

"Are they any good?" Adam asked, kind of just for something to say. Jeff shrugged.

Trey was holding Krystina loosely around the waist. I glanced anxiously at Jeff. I also couldn't think of anything to say.

"So, Jeff," I said, before I'd decided what would come next, then I just said the first thing that came into my head: "Do you think there's somewhere I could sit down for a bit?" It was totally the wrong thing to say, because Jeff is always completely over the top with worrying about me if I so much as cough or admit that I'm even slightly tired.

"Let's find a quiet spot," he said.

Adam and I followed him to a grassy square behind the apartments where the music was muted. It had been so loud a minute before that I had a steady rough hiss in my ears now that it had stopped. We sat on the grass and Jeff gave me a bottle of water. "Are you okay?" he asked.

I nodded. I was thinking, *Stop, Jeff! Don't say something crazy and concerned, something that will make Adam ask questions. Stop looking so worried about me.*

"I think we might head off soon," Adam said. He looked at me. "You think?"

"Yeah," I said. I really wanted to go, but I didn't want to leave my brother behind.

Adam and I looked at each other, then he turned to Jeff.

"Do you wanna come with us?" I felt so embarrassed, not really understanding what everyone was feeling right now.

"No, I'm sticking around," Jeff said, with a forced breeziness. "But yeah, you two go, that's smart. I'll let Krys know. I've got my phone, Liv. Call me if you need me—it doesn't matter what time it is."

I felt for my phone and took it out of my bag to show Jeff, even though he hadn't asked to see it. "Yep, I will," I said brightly.

"Are you okay?" Jeff asked again.

"I'm great!"

"Okay, you want to keep going through there, that'll get you back on the road," Jeff said, pointing the way home. We all stood up untidily, and I brushed a little dried mud off the back of Jeff's elbow. "Look after yourselves." Then Jeff headed back to the party.

"Maybe I should stay with him," I said to Adam.

"No," Adam said.

"But he was on his own."

"She won't dance all night."

"Yeah, but, it just seemed like . . ."

"I don't know Jeff the way you do, but I know blokes pretty well," Adam said. "If he and Krystina are having some kind of . . . anything . . . he's going to be really embarrassed having his little sister around to see it."

"But we're not really just brother and sister, we're more like mates," I said.

"It doesn't really work like that," Adam said. "Your sister's your sister. I'm not saying you're not as close as friends, it's better than that. But there are things you don't want your sister around for, even when you're close to her."

"What do you mean, 'things'?" I asked. "What do you think's going on?"

"Nothing. I don't know anything about it—whether it's nothing or not nothing—I just think we should leave them to it."

"What is this 'it' you keep talking about? How can 'it' be nothing? You seem to know what 'it' it is you're talking about."

Adam chuckled.

"Do I sound crazy?" I said.

"A *tiny* bit," he said, putting his finger and thumb a centimeter apart.

"I'm just worried," I said, finally smiling and bumping him with my shoulder.

Adam turned and leaned down to kiss me without holding me. I kissed him back, and we were just reaching towards each other, our lips together. It was a pretty way to kiss, although part of me was hoping he'd scoop my waist towards him and crush me with his arms.

"So let's go," I said.

"Back to yours?"

"What about that alternative plan you mentioned yesterday, your brother's balcony? The shooting stars?" I said. "Unless he's using it?"

"No, he's in Philadelphia tonight," Adam said. "Seeing his new girlfriend." He paused. "Does that change things? I don't want to make you feel uncomfortable."

"No, it doesn't," I said. But his question, even though it hadn't sounded creepy at all, had thrown up a load of all-new fears for me.

They were:

1. Had Adam noticed how freaked out Jeff seemed to be when I merely told him I needed to sit down? Like, bringing me water and asking if I was okay. Will Adam ask if something is wrong and should I tell him the truth?

2. If I'm going to Adam's brother's apartment and Dougie isn't there, will he be hoping I'll have sex with him? Should I explain I'm a virgin? Should I explain that I'm a virgin because I spent a lot of time in hospital and wasn't allowed to go out, and it's not because I'm frigid? Or should I blame it on "heartbreak" after Luke, or is it bad to mention the last boy to the present boy? Or will he not mind that I'm a virgin? I genuinely don't know whether boys are supposed to like that or not now. Seventeen is not all that old to be a virgin. Boo and Pritti are still virgins. But Adam's twenty-one and he won't be.

3. If, for the purposes of fear 1 or fear 2, I mention my illness to Adam, will he be completely repulsed by my near-deathliness and change his mind about all of it, not just sex, but . . . me?

4. If I did decide to have sex—which is unlikely—and he still wanted to have sex with me—which is unlikely after all the explanations—how would I get past the real problem—not

that I'm a virgin, but that I've never come anywhere *close* to having sex, would have no idea how to go about doing it, and would be terrible at it?

5. I really hope Jeff is okay.

"What are you thinking?" Adam said.

blogplace: Inside Adam

AUGUST 3

SO, Miss Livia Stowe has left the building.

And I can't think of a single thing to say.

Just, bloody hell.

August 3: Part 2

I just took a break from typing and made myself some toast, terrified of waking Jeff up when it *p'toinged* noisily out of the toaster. I only got a couple of hours' sleep last night and feel tired all over.

How else do I feel?

I feel *everything*. I feel happy and scared and a mess and super-confident and so-nervous-I-feel-sick and giddy and restless and I-feel-like-singing-and-dancing and oh my God I love him I love him I LOVE HIM!

I didn't see a shooting star, but there was at least one. Adam dragged his brother's tattered little armchair onto the tiny balcony, and we shared it, me curled sideways on him with my head on his chest and his arm around me, and he said, "There! Now! See it?"

"No! Where?" I said.

"Where I'm pointing . . . it's gone."

I hadn't seen it. "Are you going to make a wish?" I asked him. Adam was silent, and I thought he hadn't heard me. "Are you going to make a—?"

"*Yes,*" he laughed. "I was making it."

"What did you wish?"

"You know the rules," he said. "If I tell you, it doesn't come true." I wished he'd wished for me, but I didn't get a wish.

We talked about next year. I told him I was taking a year off before university. I was still worrying about having to explain what had been going on with my life. Adam just assumed I was taking the year off for the usual sorts of reasons—to make money or go on holiday—and I borrowed facts from my friends' lives and said I was considering all the things they're doing but I hadn't decided.

The truth is, I *don't* know what I'll be doing next year. I don't know what grades I'm going to get in my A-levels—they come out soon after I get back. It's strange that, considering they were almost all I thought about for the last four months or so, now I've almost completely stopped thinking about them. Originally there was an assumption that I'd spend the year retaking them, but my teachers seem to think I might get good enough grades that, with a personal letter from the headmaster explaining that my work was interrupted, would be good enough to apply to the universities I'm interested in. I did work very hard. Feeling slightly out of things made it easy to retreat to the library most lunchtimes in the last term, and I skipped quite a few parties.

All of this means I could have a lot of time to play with, but I don't have a place at uni this year, and Dr. Kothari thinks it would be wiser to take the year off anyway, to make sure I really get better. "Students typically forget to look after their health in their first year," she said.

Adam has one year to go—his course is four years, like Jeff's. And what we hedged around saying was that if we just happened to want to start getting serious about each other, and we just happened to decide to go for it, we'd somehow managed to coincidentally be able to see each other without either of us having to be very far away, for the whole of next year. Adam was worried about me missing the chance to use my year out to travel the world.

"I wouldn't be doing that," I said, searching the sky for another shooting star that would take his mind off the conversation.

"I think you shouldn't give up a chance like that."

"Really, look, we shouldn't talk about this anymore. We won't have to think about it for ages."

But the fact that he was talking about it, that he was *worrying* about it, told me what I'd been dying to hear. That Adam was taking me as seriously as I was taking him. I wasn't just imagining it. We'd found each other. This wasn't just a holiday romance. *So go on, Livia,* I was thinking, *tell him. Let him in.*

"Adam," I said. "There's tons of stuff you don't know about me, and it doesn't really matter, but it sort of does. I mean, it doesn't have to matter, but it might."

"You've got a boyfriend?" Adam asked quietly.

I sat upright sharply and looked him in the eyes. "No!" I said. "Well, I hope I have."

"You have." He laughed. "But not back home?"

"No!"

"So, what?"

I shut my eyes and put my head back on his chest. I didn't want to see his face for this. I didn't want to watch as his feelings for me changed. Or to see the pity cover his face like a mask, knowing that he'd still like me, probably still want to be "friends," but he wouldn't think of me the same way anymore. I wouldn't be cute and funny and fanciable anymore. I'd be brave and strange and tainted with the smells of hospitals and sickness, and he'd wonder, even though his brain told him otherwise, whether he could catch it from me.

"Okay, listen," I began, "I wish I didn't have to talk about this now, or ever, but especially now because you really don't need to have this kind of thing dumped on you when you've only just met me, basically. . . ."

"Livia, you've gone all wordy on me. Is this something to do with your leukemia? Are you getting sicker again?"

I suddenly couldn't breathe.

"*Yes. No.* How do you know about that?" I managed to ask.

"Well . . . Jeff talked about you quite a lot at uni, because he was missing you all the time. But to be honest—God, is this insensitive?—I just didn't really associate *that* Jeff's sister with *this* Jeff's sister when I met you. You're so happy and easygoing and, you know, extremely good looking. I just keep forgetting. And I didn't bring it up because I didn't know how much you wanted to talk about it."

"You've always known?"

"Well, yeah. I just . . . I don't know, I thought maybe you were sick of talking about it."

"I was scared of talking about it. I thought you wouldn't fancy me if you knew."

"If I knew what?" Adam said. "Just tell me."

"If you knew about the leukemia," I said.

"What about it?"

"Just *about* it!"

Adam grabbed hold of my shoulders. "Just *about* it? That's all? Not that you have to leave for a year to go into hospital again?"

"No, *no*. I've been all clear for a year."

"So, what are we talking about?" Adam said. "You thought I wouldn't fancy you if I found out you'd had leukemia?"

I lifted my chin. "Well?"

Adam kissed me, stroking my hair, tracing the edge of my face with his fingers, holding me really close, and my eyes were shut, but I could feel tears starting to spill through the lids.

"I'm really crazy about you," he whispered, kissing the tears on my cheeks. "For the record, I fancy you very much. Now, in the interests of full disclosure, do I have to confess to my flat feet and the mono I had when I was thirteen?"

I sent Jeff a text at about one a.m. because I didn't want to go home, and I didn't want Jeff to worry. It was starting to get too chilly to sit out on the balcony, although it was still too warm inside, and we left the windows open. Adam told me how he and his brother made their first computer when they were kids, out of old calculators and cardboard boxes.

"Wow, did it work?" I said.

Adam tilted his head on one side and grinned. "Yeah, but, as its central mechanism was a completely hollow shoe box, we had problems configuring the software to go with it."

"Oh, fine, make fun of me," I said. "Well, you're a pair of computer geniuses, aren't you? Who knows what you could do with shoe boxes?"

"We did attach little working LED lights to it. It would have fooled a lot of people."

"It's good that you still get on so well," I said. "I used to worry about losing touch with my brother when he left home. There was a time when I used to constantly be writing in my diary, *Today was probably the last time Jeff and I will ever talk like this on the phone* . . . and now that all seems stupid because we've never been closer."

"Are you still writing your blog?" Adam asked.

I flushed. Ahem: am I? Look at it, it's practically a novel. "Yes," I said. "I've been keeping up with it most nights."

"Oh, so does my, er . . . Does my name come up at all?"

"No," I said, completely deadpan. Then I smiled. "Well, I think I might have mentioned you in passing. You came with me on my New York trip, right?"

"Did I tell you I started my own blog?"

"Really? Can I read it? I mean, is it open to the public?"

"No. I just wanted to see what the appeal was. I've discovered I'm not very good at writing."

"Well, *I'm* not—you don't have to be. You just have to be good at telling the truth about yourself."

"You're good at working out what that is," Adam said. "I think not everyone can read people as well as you. You always seem to be good at getting me. I don't feel 'got' all that often."

"I've never been good at it before," I said. "I never know

what people are really thinking. I was clueless about my last boyfriend. I thought I knew him, but actually the more he knew about me, the less he liked."

Oops, I thought. Don't mention the last boyfriend to the new boyfriend. *Especially* not that he liked you less the more he knew you.

"Is he the one who made you afraid to talk about yourself?" Adam asked.

"Yeah."

"He's an idiot." Adam shook his head and stretched back, smiling. "I could listen to you talking about yourself all day. I honestly think I could never get tired of listening to you. Are you still . . . Do you still think about him a lot?"

"You mean am I over him? *Yes,* I am."

We talked most of the night lying side by side on his brother's sofa, and eventually I had to rest my eyes and I could hear my voice sounding slow and stupid and Adam's getting more distant until I was turning things he said into dialogue in a dream. I woke up at about six thirty and he was asleep. I tiptoed to the bathroom and took a look at myself. I looked quite a lot like a lunatic: mascara around my eyes, my lips dry and bright pink (very possibly from snogging a lot), my hair matted and sticking up all over my head. I could see myself more like a stranger might, in that unfamiliar mirror: the freckles standing out on my skin as if I were seeing them for the first time.

I feel as though I'm changing. Growing. I think I'd made myself a bit crazy overthinking the sex issue recently, and now, today, I feel that whatever happens is just going to happen and be easy. I just feel somehow calm now, and happy, not so anxious anymore.

When Adam woke up, he looked disorientated, and then he saw me and smiled, and he seemed to *relax*.

"Morning," he said. "Did you sleep?"

"Yeah." My voice croaked, from overuse the night before.

"Are you feeling okay?"

"Yeah, yeah."

"Er . . . do you think you're going to say anything other than 'yeah' this morning?"

I smiled, and then nodded. "Yeah."

"You look . . . a bit mad. You look very pretty, though."

"No, just mad. I've already seen myself."

"Hey, shh," Adam said. "You look beautiful. Thanks for staying. I didn't want to . . . you know, I was really happy to keep talking to you."

"Me, too. I should go, though," I said.

The early mist filtered that icing-sugary morning light I love, and there was a dewy honeysuckle scent in the air. I was wearing Adam's waffle-cotton shirt over my T-shirt and jeans, and I'd calmed my hair into two braids, the ends fastened with tiny rubber bands I'd found in Adam's brother's flat. A couple of joggers ran past us, panting and talking to each other. The weird diner made out of an old bank was already quite bustling, and I could smell pancakes as we walked by the door. I suddenly felt hungry, and my tiredness caught up with me as if I'd just put on a heavy coat. I kept sneaking little glances at Adam just because I wanted to see his face, because his face made me happy. We were holding hands, and I realized that my hands didn't feel sweaty at all.

We kissed outside the door, and whispered our good-byes.

"Do you fancy doing something a bit later?" I asked. It crossed my mind that this sounded too keen, and I should have let him ask me, and then, according to some romance guides, I should have turned him down. But I didn't really care. It just doesn't feel right to play who-cares-less games with Adam. It's a waste of our time.

"Yes," he said. "I might go back and sleep for another couple of hours. But call me anytime you want."

We looked at each other. We just couldn't seem to let go. *Come on, Livia,* I was thinking, *you look terrible, get inside, do yourself a favor. Call him later when your hair is nice.* This logic finally won me round, and I kissed him once more and went in.

blogplace: Inside Adam

AUGUST 3: PART 2

JUST, BLOODY HELL. I love her.

August 7

It's been a few days since I updated my blog, but look, I've been busy. It's been *more* than a few days since I updated my "Things I Know," so that's what I'm going to start with.

Things I know about love.

1. Nothing that happens between two people is guaranteed to be private.

2. Strangers are called strangers because they are *strange.* Duh!

(These are Unshakeable Truths.)

3. People don't always tell you the truth about how they feel. And the truth is, it may not be the same as how you feel. *And girls can be as guilty of this as boys.*

4. Hearts don't really get broken, but if you practice too hard with them, they can get quite hurt. It feels like they won't get better, but they do.

5. I am in it.

The bad news first. Krystina told Jeff that she was now seeing Trey, the musician guy she'd been dancing with at the party. Jeff said he must have read the signs wrongly because Krystina "seemed surprised" that Jeff thought they were going out. This made me *so angry*. It's one thing to dump my brother, but another to pretend you didn't even dump him. She was snogging him on the sofa in this very flat, and yes, sometimes a snog means nothing, but when the snoggee is as into you as my brother was into Krystina, and you know it—and she *knew* it!—you have to respect their feelings a bit more. You can't just go around saying, "Oh, were you serious about that? Really? How funny, I snog all my friends," or whatever Krystina said. Jeff didn't want to talk about it, and was only answering my question about what was going on between them and I wish I hadn't asked.

But Jeff has been pretty blue since this happened, and I only have six more days in Princeton and I don't want Jeff to be moping all the time. That sounds really selfish: I don't mean it to be about me. It's just that I feel useless, but as I'm spending more time with him than I ever have before, I feel that I ought to be use*ful*. I'm worried that I'm annoying him by being upbeat and chirpy. I'm worried that I'm having this stupid, exciting romance with Adam in his face all the time.

Yesterday, I'd arranged to go for a picnic by Lake Carnegie with Adam but I called him to cancel, and said I wanted to spend the day with Jeff. I didn't explain why, but Adam totally got it, and was really sweet. Jeff and I went to see a pretty bad comedy at the cinema in the shopping mall—and then we came home and made a chili together from scratch. This may seem like a slightly insane thing to make when it's so hot out, but Jeff wanted to prove he was good at making it, and said people in hot countries ate the hottest food, and we had a really good time. Jeff showed me how to wash your hands with oil before cutting the actual chili peppers, so they don't burn your skin. We baked some bread to go with it—weird sort of bread, kind of like scones—that one of his American friends had taught him to make. We turned the stereo up really loudly and rocked to it as we chopped and kneaded and baked and, for the first time in a couple of days, everything seemed to go back to normal, and it was like we were kids again, working hard together on something.

Although, something happened in the middle of all this that wasn't so normal, or nice. Jeff had sent me out to get some cumin seeds for the top of the bread. I went to the little outdoors mini mall where there's a very posh food shop which sells that sort of thing, and I saw Krystina. She was alone. I gasped as if I'd seen a ghost, and then panicked about what I was going to say to her. The last time we'd talked, I'd been dancing with her at a party and she'd been my fantastic new friend. A few days later, should I just act as though nothing was different? Should I be cool with her, or disapproving—confront her or make a big deal out of letting her know I forgave her? I hadn't forgiven her.

I didn't have to make the choice. Krystina saw me—our eyes met properly, there was no mistake—and she turned in the other direction and vanished into the DVD-rental shop. I didn't follow her in, of course. I mean, maybe she was as nervous or as embarrassed as I was. I just stood there, sort of paralyzed and feeling dizzy, my heart beating as if I'd had a real scare. I was so upset that I forgot all about the cumin seeds, and when I got home I had to lie to Jeff and tell him they didn't have any. I didn't say I'd seen Krystina.

When we'd made our chili, we put on the webcam to talk to Mum. It was late at her end, and she was wearing pajamas.

"So, are you feeling ready to come home?" she asked me. "Or have you fallen in love with America, too?"

Not with America, I thought. But. I'm just saving it. I've talked about him, obviously, but I'm going to *really* tell her all about Adam when I get back. If I tell her now, she'll only find something new to worry about.

"I'm missing you," I said.

"Oh, I suppose that means you'll be getting the plane back next week, then?" Mum said. My God, it really was just a week away. "I'm afraid I've already sublet your room—I'll have to give the new tenant notice." Jeff just laughed; he doesn't take jokes too seriously, but he does indulge my mum's weak ones.

"Could you also make sure you have lots of Cadbury's chocolate in the cupboard? I'm missing it," I said. "This Hershey's stuff is—"

"Are you getting a cold?" Mum asked suddenly. My voice was croaky again, as it had been on and off since the night of the Butler party, when I'd had to shout over the loud music.

"No, it's just a sore throat," I said.

"How sore?"

"No, I just mean croaky. It's not sore."

"Are you taking your pills?" Mum demanded.

"Of course I am."

Just when I'm having a normal conversation with Mum,

she will always remember to slip back into Classic Mum, which involves treating me like a five-year-old, or an idiot, or both.

"Jeff, is she okay?" Mum shouted.

"We've been tasting the chili," Jeff said. "It's pretty strong. It might have taken a layer off her throat."

"I just worry, Livia," Mum said, going all honest.

"I know."

"And I miss you a lot."

"I miss you, too, Mum. I can't wait to see you," I said, wanting to cry.

"Hey, what about me?" Jeff shouted from the other side of the room.

"You, too," Mum said. "I wish you'd both come home."

"We'll be home soon," I said. "Me first."

AUGUST 8

IT'S WEIRD how you think you've got your life sussed and then it flips over and all your priorities change. A few weeks ago I was dreading going back to England because I've got to knock the Java project into shape for submission for the course, which means work work work. The work will still be there, but now, going back is suddenly more about taking Livia to my favorite places, and meeting my mates at home and introducing her as my girlfriend.

She still has a few days in Princeton, but I don't go back till the twenty-fifth, which means two weeks without her. I'm going to miss her, it's as simple as that. No, it's not as simple as that. I am going to really miss her. We've got a breakfast routine now, you know—we're supposed to meet for coffee every morning at nine, but both of us always show up about ten minutes early. I've never known a girl who's always early: I'd always worked on the theory that lateness is taught to women in PE at school, when the classes are split girl/boy. Livia has as much reason to be late as any other girl—more actually, seeing as how she's funny and beautiful and I'd wait three hours for her. So it's endearingly . . . *geeky* of her that she never is. I am aware that in any official classification system, I would be a geek and she would be a hottie, but I am quite a cool *geek*—and only technically a geek, being a techie—and she is quite a nerdy hottie, having some kind of mild *Star Trek* obsession and a slightly disturbing knowledge of every British sci-fi series made in the last century.

I love that about her.

And she's only *technically* a hottie, her claim to the term being exclusively composed of her gorgeous face and body, and having hair like a sunset over a cornfield on the longest day of summer. Apart from that, she's giggly and clumsy and shy at the most unexpected times.

And always early.

It means I always have to be even earlier just so I can stand outside the coffee shop and watch her walking towards me. I think there's nothing in the world I like as much as the sight of Livia Stowe walking towards me, and the way she always looks as if she's trying not to smile, and then gives in.

The first time I went to New York with Livia I was trying (too hard) to show off how hip I was, so I took her round the ultra-trendy districts and the kind of places only New Yorkers know about. We're going again on Wednesday and I think we should do it differently this time. My new plan is to go about it like a proper tourist, find out the places Livia thinks of when she thinks of New York, and try to head for all of the clichés, in a good way. For one thing, because I've only been with my brother before and he hasn't got any patience for that kind of thing, I haven't really been to any of the "big" places myself—you know, like the Empire State Building, MoMa, Grand Central Station, and whatever. So for selfish reasons, I would really love to see these places for the first time with Livia, and not waste my next time there with her being all, like, seen-it-done-it-bought-the-pretzel. However, me being me, I can't be totally spontaneous, so I'm spending the morning working out the most efficient route for seeing any combination of sights Livia might happen to mention, and linking that to corresponding places to stop for lunch or coffee, and I'll print that out and take it with us when we go.

I might still pretend to Livia that I'm making it up as I go along. As I said, I am quite a cool geek. I've got to think of my image.

August 9

I am not feeling great today, to be honest. I can't seem to shake off this sore throat. Jeff has said he thinks I should see a doctor. I don't think that's necessary yet, but I will soon if it doesn't improve, just to be safe. Rationally, I know that nothing is wrong, but I'm so used to getting checked out at home, and what with not being near my mum and all of us being slightly more nervous and careful than we usually are, if I don't have it confirmed that everything's exactly as it should be I'll start imagining I'm feeling worse than I am. What I think, though, is that I'm going back on the twelfth anyway, so the sensible thing to do is wait till then, and see people who know me, rather than spend three hours filling in my medical history and insurance forms and waiting in a waiting room, all for a sore throat.

We went out in a large group this evening—some of the American students Jeff's been taking a history class with, Jeff, Adam, and me. One of the other boys, Carl, was flirting with me, and I didn't know if I'd walked in looking as though I was with Adam. When you're at school, everyone knows who everyone else is going out with. I was pretty sure Carl was trying to chat me up but it's hard to know when to say, "Oh, sorry, I'm with someone already." If you say it too early, you could find out he wasn't chatting you up at all, and you've made a fool of yourself being big-headed enough to tell him to back off. If you say it too late, you're worried you've wasted his time. Some boys get embarrassed and angry about any kind of rejection at all, and sort of blow up at you if you tell them you're not interested, no matter when and how you say it. As I was tying myself into knots wondering how I should talk to Carl and whether it was flirty to laugh at his jokes, I caught Adam's eye. Adam raised his eyebrows an *almost* invisible amount and smiled at me. It was like he was saying, "Don't worry, you won't fall. I've got you." My skin seemed to tingle, as if my happiness was sparkling all over me like the fizz above a freshly poured lemonade. I lowered my chin and smiled back at him; it was a smile just for the two of us. Then I carried on talking to Carl.

Jeff was looking at the door a lot. I think he was worried that Krystina would walk in with Trey, the band boy, or even without him, and he'd have to see her, or speak to her, whatever—but react in some way. Jeff's sort of okay-ish. Well, he's still a bit quiet and he's still not talking about Krystina, but he's started making jokes again. He was very, very into her for a long time before they kissed, but *after* they had, their relationship didn't go on very long, so I think it was better that it happened now, before he properly fell in love with her. For one thing, Saira always told me that the longer you go out with someone, the longer it takes to get over breaking up with them. What Saira literally says is that it takes exactly *half* the time you go out with a boy to get over him. Back when I was still overanalyzing every moment of my romance with Luke, I used this equation to work out when I'd stop caring about him. For the record, it doesn't work—the math is wrong—but it does make sense that the longer you were seeing them, the longer it takes to feel normal again when they're not in your life.

The other thing is, and this is new to me so it may not be true, but I believe you only *start* falling in love with someone when you know they feel the same way about you. That's when you start to trust them. So you relax and stop thinking about yourself, because you're not worried about getting it wrong and losing them. When you stop thinking constantly about yourself, it frees up all your spare time to think about how utterly, perfectly perfect they are and how lucky you are to have found them. Yowza, that really is how I feel. Yeek. Unrequited love is like buying a dress that you can't fit into but you promise yourself you'll diet for—you can't think about the dress, only about the fact that your body is too big for it. Unrequited love can give you butterflies and tingly lips and lovely, dizzy days where you analyze every word of every sentence they've ever said to you . . . but you cry a lot, too. Proper being in love isn't the same: it feels safe, but the opposite of boring. It's deep; you're jumping into the waterfall.

I think my lovely brother hasn't been in too deep this time. That's why he'll be okay.

I'm going to New York again with Adam tomorrow. We

asked Jeff if he wanted to come. We weren't just being nice or anything: I think being in New York City with my brother and Adam would make me happier than just about anything in the world. I tried really hard to change his mind, but Jeff says he has to get everything he can out of the libraries before he goes back, because they're so much better for American history than the one in Manchester. I hope that's true. I hope he's not just ducking out because he's so unhappy, or worse, because he thinks he'll be in the way or something mad like that. But after New York, I still have one full day and night left in Princeton before I go home, and Jeff has promised to drop all books and let his hair down. I'm going to remind him, and I'm going to make him.

Our rough plan for tomorrow is to act like tourists. Adam's asked me to come up with a list of things that I think of when I think of New York, and I can't make up my mind. Central Park, definitely. Macy's or Barneys or Saks or Bloomingdale's? Broadway at night, maybe? I love that it's so warm right now that you never feel cold in the evening, and the daylight lasts and lasts until the sun sets, which start off like fresh pink rose petals until the sky seems to tear in half, light and dark. Oh, Grand Central Station—it sounds so romantic and looks so beautiful when you see it in films. The thought of going back into Manhattan is giving me such jitters, in a good way, that I might not sleep tonight. It's nearly midnight now and I don't feel tired at all. We're setting off really early. I've got a paper note here on my desk, and Adam has written on it, *Wear sensible shoes!* and on the other side he's added, *And a short skirt.*

Things I know about love.

1. Being
2. In
3. Love
4. Is
5. The
6. Best
7. Thing
8. In
9. The
10. World.

August 10

6:19 a.m. Throat still hurts. I'm worried that I'm feeling a bit woozy still, but I've been feeling woozy practically since I got here, and at first it was jetlag, and then it was sunstroke, and this time, I just think it's a couple of late nights. Should I tell Jeff? If I tell Jeff, the jig is up. Jeff will insist I stay home and rest and we call out a doctor. I'm flying home in less than two days. I don't have time to rest. But I think I will tell Adam I don't feel great. I'll tell him when we're on the train.

I have my list. Grand Central Station is on it, because last time I assumed the Princeton train would go straight there, and was a *little* bit disappointed when it took us to a modern station in a kind of ordinary shopping mall—it's called Penn Station. I want to see the one you see in films. Then there's Central Park, Bloomingdale's, the Museum of Natural History and the Planetarium, the Empire State Building, and tea at the Algonquin Hotel.

I just feel a bit . . . like when I close my eyes for more than a second and open them again, my brain has started to fall down through my body and it has to hurry up to the top of my head to get back to business. The only reason I'm even slightly worried about this is because the last time I had a persistent sore throat, you know what happened.

Look at my list! It could be a year, it could be *years* before I have another chance to see those things. Whatever is wrong with me—and it might just be hypochondria—It. Can. Wait. Because I can't.

August 11

Mum's on her way. She'll be here some time in the early morning. I know she won't show it, but I know how angry she'll be: blaming herself for letting me come here, blaming me for not looking out for the signs earlier or telling someone. This was the last thing I wanted in the world, hurting my mum again when it could have been prevented and she's been through so much with me already. I feel better today, but I've been told I'm worse, that I only feel better because they've controlled my fever. This isn't my computer—Jeff didn't bring my computer. There's a computer room here in the hospital and they said I was allowed ten minutes to check my e-mails. I told them I really needed to check my e-mails. Marigold, the film-star beautiful Japanese nurse, has pushed me here in a wheelchair and is standing with her back against the wall, reminding me that I only have five minutes, and not to tire myself. It's ten minutes, Marigold, *ten*, and what else am I going to do all night? They sent Jeff and Adam away about half an hour ago, but they're staying in a hotel nearby, and not going back to Princeton.

I don't have any time to write, and I don't know which order to write in. I can't believe this. I'm scared and ANGRY because THIS WAS NOT THE TIME FOR THIS TO HAPPEN! I have to stop looking so angry while I'm typing because Marigold is looking. I keep smashing the keys and sighing. I have to calm down.

Calmly, then, my white cells are up a lot. I knew it as soon as I saw their faces; it's a look I've seen before. The tests confirmed it.

We were on the train to New York and I was resting my head on Adam's shoulder.

"Are you okay?" he asked me.

"It's just the early start," I said, and shivered.

He held my hand and I was aware that it felt cold and clammy, so I pretended I needed to fix my hair.

"Well, let's go slowly today. Anyway, it's too hot to do everything," Adam said, and I felt sad all over, and was determined not to let anything else show.

By the time we'd got off the train, I was feeling really energetic again, although I was trying not to talk too much because my throat was dry. The first place we went was Grand Central Station, which made me speechless anyway. It's so beautiful, almost like a palace, and the ceilings are painted like the night sky, with golden stars set on navy blue. Walking into the station straight from a bright, sweaty New York morning is like walking into the past.

Marigold is saying I should come back to bed. I have to hurry.

If Adam hadn't left me alone I might have been able to keep faking, but we split up for about a half hour because he said he really needed to get some extra hard-disk space for his brother's computer and he had to get it from the Apple shop and he wouldn't be long and he didn't want to drag me with him when he could just do it quickly. At the time I thought this was a brilliant idea, because we'd been walking down Fifth Avenue and I needed a rest. There was no real reason I needed a rest, because we were walking on the shady side of the street. I told him I hadn't really worn my most comfortable shoes because they didn't go with my short skirt. Adam found us the sweetest little coffee shop, all bent-wood chairs and chocolate cakes with raspberry pink icing, and sat me down with an iced tea and some pistachio cookies and said he'd be back soon. He did come back quickly, but by this time, I'd sat long enough with nothing else to think about and realized how I felt and that I felt horrible. But even then I just couldn't tell him. I'm such an *idiot*.

Our next stop was FAO Schwarz, which is the fanciest toy shop in the world, and appears in a film I once saw called *Big*, where the main character dances on a giant piano and plays "Chopsticks" while he dances. We just meant to basically walk straight through it on our way to Central Park, where our plan was to lie in the cool, damp shade and watch New Yorkers for a couple of hours, and eat ice cream, and read our books and pretend we lived here. I knew I could handle that. We were wandering through the shop and everything was so beautiful and I wanted to touch it all, but I was looking at a wall of fluffy soft jungle animals, like giant furry tigers and lions, and I suddenly had the feeling that the wall was going to come down on me and I couldn't stand up anymore and then I must have fainted. When I came to, I was lying down, and instead of the furry tigers and lions looking at me, there were now lots of strange, loud faces, people I didn't know crowding me, and I was completely disoriented, and shivering so much that it felt like I had frostbite, and I told Adam I'd better get to a hospital.

His face. I felt like a *fraud*. Guilty. As if I'd been fooling him by not telling him the truth about how bad I'd been feeling. Adam looked terrified—he was white and swallowing a lot. He said he'd called Jeff. I said, "Don't call Jeff!" weakly, but I was so glad Jeff was coming. Then Adam lifted me up and I held his neck and I was terrified, because you go through life hardly ever being lifted and it's disorienting—moving too quickly without doing any part of it yourself. I held on to his shoulders, and he carried me outside the shop, where there was a cab waiting somehow, maybe the shop had called it, and we drove to a hospital. He held my hand so tightly while we waited, and while I was trying to explain my medical history to the ER nurse, and when I was transferred to a wheelchair. Adam still held me, and when I had to go alone down into the ward for tests, he leaned close to me and put his arms around me and whispered, "I love you." I said, "I'm okay. Don't worry. I'm sorry, I'm so sorry," and he whispered again, "I love you. Shh."

Please, Marigold, just another couple of minutes. I know I can come back later, but I want to write this when it's fresh in my mind. I don't want to forget. I believe everything Adam tells me, all the things his eyes say as well as his lips, but even the truest, best guy would be forgiven for watching this kind of thing happen to me and thinking, *Enough, too much, I need to get away.*

So what I feel right now, I want to write about while it's still as pure and real as it ever will be. Before life comes in with its big clumsy feet and stamps all over my heart.

I love him.

This doesn't feel like the loves I've known before, the boys who've made me cry and filled my diaries. We're not playing games—holding back and pretending that we don't really care, or that we really do. We just like to spend every minute together, and the days burn up as fast as matches and it's me and him together talking, and laughing, and talking, and holding each other, and knowing it's right. When I'm in his arms, sometimes the emotions feel too big for me and I want to cry. It makes me afraid because I'm so *happy*, and the future is *huge* and in front of us, and I can't believe I might spend it with Adam. I'm so angry with myself for getting ill again—I don't have time for it.

blogplace: Inside Adam

AUGUST 12

LIVIA'S MUM blames me. Jeff introduced us and you could see her thinking, *Oh, right, you're the one. It's you who took her into the middle of New York and let her get sick without even noticing. Lovely to meet you.* She's spent every second with Livia. Livia was crying and asking for her mum before she arrived and I was so glad she was here because I just wanted my baby to be happy and feel better and get better. But as soon as she did, I realized that I had to stand a lot farther back. I ended up stuck in a corridor for hours, staring at my hands. I was suddenly aware of my T-shirt being worn and sweaty. A thousand people walked up and down and most of them looked at me as if they were wondering why I was there.

AUGUST 14

THE NEXT DAY, the nurse told me Livia was sitting up and feeling better, and Jeff came out and asked me if I wanted to see her. It seemed like a bit of a nuts question as I'd been there since six a.m. I had the shoes with me, the little red Dorothy shoes I bought her just before she collapsed, and I was going to tell her that when she was feeling a bit better she could put them on and tap her heels together to get home. But then I saw her and she didn't look better. She was wired up to an IV unit, with something dripping into the back of her hand. Jeff and Livia's mum left us alone.

"I'm really sorry about this," Livia said. "I usually like to wait till I really get to know a guy before I start nearly dying in front of him."

I tried to laugh. "I love you," I said.

"I love you," she said.

We sat in silence for a few seconds and I wanted to cry.

"So when are you getting out?" I said. I was trying to sound upbeat.

"I don't know," Livia said, and started doing a really scary cough. "Sorry, the antibiotics are supposed to be sorting that out." She waved her hand, and the wire to the IV unit shook. "Ow," she said.

"Does it hurt?"

"No, it's just the thingy in my hand. It's a bit tender."

"I should have noticed you were ill. I should never have taken you so far."

"Adam, this isn't your fault."

"It is my fault."

Livia's eyes went all teary and I changed the subject, I don't remember what to. I sort of remember we talked about Princeton and Manchester and Jeff and songs and a kids' TV show we both used to watch and it *sounded* like us, but

148

underneath the talk we were desperate to hold each other and couldn't.

"What's in the bag?" Livia said.

"Oh. Nothing," I said. I was suddenly ashamed of what I'd bought, because it reminded me of leaving her alone in New York. Livia nodded, and said okay. So I took them out, because I didn't have anything nice to give her. I mumbled words that didn't really mean anything while I opened the box. Livia started crying properly, which wasn't the reaction I'd planned on getting. I was terrified her mum would come back in and tell me off for upsetting her and chase me out, throwing the shoes at my head one by one. Livia swung her feet out of the bed. She was wearing little blue-checked pajamas, and she'd rolled the legs up. Her legs, you know, so utterly sexy. It was entirely inappropriate but I was just thinking, *Woah, you've got seriously great legs, Livia,* even though I'd obviously seen them before. She slipped the shoes on, and then wiped her eyes with her pajama sleeve.

"They're lovely," she said. Her voice cracked, then she started crying again, and coughing, again, and I helped her to lie back down. Her skin was cold and goose-bumpy, and she felt so light.

"When you get out of here, I'll take you on an unreasonably long walk in them," I said, and kissed her face through her tears.

"You're always telling me to wear sensible shoes."

"Oh, screw that," I said. "I like it when you look beautiful."

"You can't like me much now, then," Livia whispered.

"You're beautiful and sexy now, and I love you now—I

149

love you, Livia." I squeezed her hands, worrying that I was hurting the one with the drip in it. "You believe that, don't you?"

She nodded. "Yes."

"I wish I could take you out of this place." My voice broke. I dropped my head on the sheet, near her lap.

"Don't leave yet," Livia said. She stroked my hair. I wanted to grab her to me.

"I'm not going anywhere."

This is going to sound odd . . . but a small part of me was happy, sitting with her there. I was thinking, *Now we've done everything together—like the hard thing, as well as the fun things. We're an item, we're solid. We're together.*

Livia died in her sleep that night.

When I came in the morning after, at seven, I was told that she'd developed pneumonia and the antibiotics hadn't controlled it. I asked what that meant. It took me ages to understand what they were telling me, that she was dead. I kept saying, "So what happens now?" until the nurse said, "I'm afraid she died, sir," and I tried to swallow and my throat seemed to block up with dry hairs and I started choking. I was *furious* with Jeff for not calling me and getting me in earlier, but I knew that was stupid and selfish of me. Jeff was going through what he was going through. Livia would have wanted her family around her. But I loved her, too.

I thought they didn't care and couldn't see that, and had stopped thinking about me altogether, and I was angry with them and started practicing things I'd never say to them about how much I loved her. Livia's mum appeared at the edge of the ward, came up to me, and I couldn't read her expression at all, I thought she might shake me, or hit me, or shout at me, and at that moment I realized I really wanted that—to be blamed and told off, to focus all the guilt and anger I felt at myself.

But Livia's mum hugged me. Really hard, for a lady—I almost had trouble breathing. I said, "I'm so sorry. I would have done anything not to hurt her." I felt really young, as if she was my mum and I needed her to comfort me, and I closed my eyes and held on as if my life depended on it.

AUGUST 15

LET ME tell you something. I don't believe in love at first sight. I don't believe in soul mates or that there's one person who's just right for you and all that bullshit. I don't believe in any of it. If it's all true, and I fell in love with Livia the first time I saw her smudged-makeup-y face back in Manchester, and the world stopped turning when I looked in her eyes, and I couldn't stop thinking about her even though I didn't see her again for a year, and then I saw her again, and it was like the sun coming out from behind a cloud going, *This Is The One, THIS IS IT*—if that is all true, then *why*?

Well, of course I do believe in all of it, because it happened to me. It's stupidly self-obsessed to try and explain the important moments of your life as something that happened to make you aware of how precious life is, or that someone came into your world to show you how to feel, and I know for certain that Livia Stowe's whole life was not about making sure I had one perfect summer. Like everyone who has been in love, we just got lucky, but our luck ran out.

AUGUST 23

WHEN they find out you didn't know the love of your life for a very long time, people recalculate their sympathy. But that's fine, I don't want to talk about Livia to other people.

I've been back in England a week. I keep thinking of everything in terms of how Livia would see it and what Livia would say about it. Including Livia's funeral. I had such a clear sense of her that day, almost as if she was sitting next to me whispering in my ear, "I hate it when my mum cries. Why didn't you tell them to play the Beatles song? You know I love it. Don't cry, you'll start me off."

I'm still working on code with Dougie, only we do it over webcams now and he doesn't pick up on my mistakes as much because he's being sensitive. I've got my own Java project to do. I've got tons of things to be getting on with. Loads of people who want to take me out of myself, and loads of excuses to turn them down. I've just got to keep going and hope that one day it starts to feel not quite as bad as it does now.

I talk to Livia at night when I'm lying in bed, and I think I almost believe she can hear me. I'm careful about what I say, anyway, and I try not to cry when I remind her that she left me at the worst possible time, because I knew her enough to know I was completely in love with her, but she didn't leave me with enough memories. I'm scared of using up the few I have, and turning them into memories of memories, like songs you loved that you've played too many times, and you feel just a bit less excited by each time. And I hear my little pretend Livia, close to my ear, saying, "It really happened, Adam. I was here, and I loved you, too." Then I turn over hard, because I'm angry with the world, and my sheets feel lumpy and untidy and I do my best to fall asleep.

KATE LE VANN was born in Yorkshire, England, but has lived many places, including Princeton, New Jersey. She's written for *CosmoGIRL!*, *Vogue*, *Company*, and *The Big Issue*.

She visits New York City as often as she can but has been there twice chasing after boys. The first boy was not that into her. The second showed up to the airport an hour late because he was buying plastic spoons at Ikea and lost track of time. She married that one.

She lives in England with her husband and two daughters.